# iSly

By Stanley Gerson

First Edition

Biographical Publishing Company
Prospect, Connecticut

# iSly

## First Edition

Published by:

### Biographical Publishing Company
95 Sycamore Drive
Prospect, CT 06712-1493
Phone: 203-758-3661 Fax: 253-793-2618
e-mail: biopub@aol.com

Copyright © 2011 by Stanley Gerson
Cover art by: David Gerstmann
Second Printing 2012

PRINTED IN THE UNITED STATES OF AMERICA

Publisher's Cataloging-in-Publication Data


Gerson, Stanley.
iSly/ by Stanley Gerson.
1st ed.
p. cm.
ISBN 1-929882-64-5 (alk. Paper)
13-Digit ISBN 978-1-929882-64-9
1. Title.  2. Science fiction/fantasy. 3. American fiction.
Dewey Decimal Classification: 813 American Fiction
Library of Congress Control Number: 2011930087

# Table of Contents

". . . success or failure, life or death, have no meaning to androids. Why should they matter to humans?"

Hive Main

# Chapter 1
## The Greens

The bogie appeared on Slade's radar screen; it was a wonder. Slade Raleigh was assigned to the Air Force, Early Warning Station, secreted away on a hill northwest of Washington D.C.

"Bogie approaching at 10 o'clock, Commander Stennis. It's headed straight for the White House; its speed is mach 7, say again mach 7," Slade reported. The digital image and information were already on the Commander's transparent screen, but communications were, still, always verbalized.

The Commander grabbed a microphone by his display and hit the red button. "This is Commander Stennis speaking to Quarterback: Scramble Wraith One & Two; vector them straight to attack positions on the incoming bogie. Full fan!"

"Quarterback; roger that Commander."

Moments later Wraith One reported to the Commander: "Commander Stennis, this is Wraith One & Two coming up to speed and altitude on bogie attack positions. We await further orders."

Colonel Avery Stennis was a solid officer, with a voice that rumbled deep from his being, and he had no problems making decisions. "This is Commander Stennis and this is *not* a drill. Listen men: When that thing crosses into restricted air-space, your orders are to shoot it down immediately from your attack positions. I repeat: no bow shots, no wing waggling; waste it quick! This is not a drill. And the kill order stands unless I personally tell you men otherwise."

"Wraith One; roger that Commander," was the terse reply.

Stennis grabbed a red phone from this desk drawer. Hit the button to the forward air base that the bogie over-flew. "Commander Stennis speaking to Forward; are the scout planes up?"

"This is Forward. Scout planes are up and we have a visual."

"What!"

"No markings Commander; no transponder signal. It appears to be an advanced jet fighter, unknown to us. Repeat: It's alien."

"Stennis out." Phone hung up he seized the microphone, "Wraith One & Two, I'm changing the rules of engagement: Come to attack positions and shoot that aircraft down. Don't worry which airspace it's in. I repeat, shoot it down instantly."

- - - - ◇ - - - -

The Greens had cratered . . . but now top leaders were ending up there: from the military, government, and business. Dignitaries.

Joseph Dane studied the passing scenes, riding passenger. This was his third trip to the Greens, but its stark conditions and tried humanity had never hit him with bigger impact. Conditions were getting desperate; the spike in the green numbers created deplorable conditions: Hollow logs, holes in the brush, and holes in the ground were the projects, lean-tos and caves were middle-class, and yurts were the mansions.

"Past that far hill?" the driver asked.

"Yeah," Dane breathed.

It was a still, gray February 23d morning; nothing else seemed certain.

"I'm learning how to drive, again, since we left the magstripe," the driver said, "Hope it's not too obvious."

Dane nodded, "Just don't hit anybody . . . And Bluegrass, I'm curious; how did you line up this vehicle on such short notice? I'm impressed."

"It just popped up as a lost Departmental slot," Bluegrass said, "Some old VIP reservation that got canceled."

"Uh huh," Dane said, watching for landmarks . . . *Paul Adams, alias Bluegrass: behind-the-scenes office assistant, bluegrass banjo and viola player, slight-of-hand artist, great at office parties. And man of surprises when it came to finding unique solutions*, Dane mused.

Bluegrass had degrees from Northwestern in business and finance with minors in music and literature, but he was content to work in the background at the present time. Dumb luck seemed to favor him. Bluegrass was in his late twenties and Dane knew he had a lot more going for him than " . . . success through screwing up," as the office chatter had it.

Even Dillingham, his former supervisor, was quoted as saying, "Bluegrass succeeds, but it's only by accident."

*I'd rather be lucky than good, myself*, Dane thought.

Bluegrass stole the show at the Christmas party, and the children loved him. His goofy smile was a winner in his magic act; his face was a beacon, framed by his solid, black hair, on his 5'-10" slender frame. He played the viola with passion, lilting the Christmas carols to an improv jazz beat, jamming the melody chord, lyrically hitting just enough notes to make the song recognizable. It was beautiful. He was shy in real life, but a natural showman. Bluegrass spoke with a slight southern drawl, which would get nasal and twangy if the subject were very important, or urgent.

The Demographic Services vehicle cruised past tree-lined slopes; fingers of fog had the landscape locked in winter. Hopefully there would be a few sunny days, soon. The vehicle and riders became native to their surroundings, the further on they went.

Dane hoped this trip would clear some things up. The Vice-President and a National Security Council general were slated for displacement to the Greens – that much was known. Two reputed billionaires were already there.

A significant judicial figure was already here.

To say concern was stirring in high places was an understatement – it was more like cold fear. A rogue process had spawned, and exploded as a pestilence in androids, that was taking over the Internet. This out-of-control program, a simple set of ones and zeros, could either land humanity in utopia, or in a rift, valley volcano, with ease equal to dispassion. The drift of events had national and world leaders horrified, since a new world domination by androids seemed possible.

Dane stirred, "That dirt road to the left, Bluegrass." The car slowed, turned left, and proceeded a few hundred yards up a gravel dirt road. A shanty-town emerged in a level clearing.

"Just stop by that lean-to in the middle, Blue."

"I'm seein' why you didn't try to describe this place Joe; I've seen better landfills than this spot."

"You should've seen it before it got cleaned up . . . Let's get this done," Dane said.

Bluegrass parked the car and broke the vacuum seal; both doors swung up automatically. They got out and Bluegrass pressed the fob button, closing the doors. Diseases had raged in the greens before now, and whoever ventured out, did so at his own peril. Getting quarantined was one of the lesser possibilities. So the two, professionally dressed men cast an absurd contrast to the dire scene they walked through, heading toward the lean-to.

Joe Dane was still trim – just too much gut left. He was in good physical condition and had an athletic stride. But the graying at his temples belied youthfulness. His face and blue eyes were pleasant, but reflected a maturity he'd gained from being in the pit, wrestling with life's big challenges. The soft crow's feet and facial lines were from success, from failure, from happiness, and from disaster. He'd seen it all: The good times that seemed forever, survival of crushing defeat, and back to different good times. An indefatigable confidence was building in him, stronger than ever.

Humility, patience, and hope were causing life to break in good places for Dane. His stride was confident, attitude positive, and he usually had a pleasant look on his face. He had tanned and his hair had bleached out in last summer's sun. The trail and beach jogging had done a lot of good for his 6'-3" frame; he'd be in fighting trim when it was time for it.

Dane had become a man of few words, and he'd stick to the job at hand. He carried himself like a man. His voice was adequate, strong if necessary. He usually moved through life with ease, and could offer a smile and a good word, when they were called for . . .

Yes, life was good, now, and he was getting more time to spend with his wife, Belyn. He treasured her.

The Greens community was not an unfamiliar scene to Dane; it tapped into memories of his being blackballed – hounded to the point of having no choice, but to go underground; disappear out on the street and in subways. His name, then, was Jason Dunn. Thanks to his wife, who had her own professional identity, and with help from his friends, he'd been able to establish a new address and retrain as a paralegal, with a minor in social demographics.

His new name, Joe Dane, and his life in the Office of Demographics was either under the radar, or of disinterest to his former detractors. Dane knew they had their reasons.

The irony was it'd never been about him personally . . . He wished he'd built up an alternate identity to move onto, like his former mentor. But he sure had one now. *That was then, and this is now*, he thought, shaking it all off.

*New day and don't look back.*

The lean-to was covered with an old, grim canvass with paint spots. Weeds peeked out where it hung over the walls, built up of pallets and wood sheeting. Smoke rose from a chimney set in the roadside wall. It was an obvious center for the sylvan community. A flap was pinned open for an entrance, and inside was a graying but sturdy figure of a man. He was busy handing food and a little jumpsuit to a woman holding an infant. He looked familiar to Bluegrass but he couldn't place him. The man's eyes lit up as they approached.

"Joe," he greeted, "Who's your friend?"

"Paul Adams, alias Bluegrass. Bluegrass meet Wilson Sinclair."

"Hello, Bluegrass."

Bluegrass nodded, with a start, now realizing he was talking to the former CEO of Synergy Earth, the multinational robotics company. Sinclair had been charged with *AndRan*, the huge android project which had salvaged the earth.

Wilson Sinclair reflected ability, personality, and a strength befitting of his former office. He'd started his career at Midwestern Cybernetics, where he'd first met Dane. Sinclair came up through professional sales to become CEO of Midwestern.

He was a good one; the company thrived under his leadership. When Synergy Interstate tried to consummate an unfriendly takeover of Midwestern Cybernetics, Sinclair led Midwestern on a brilliant odyssey and steady battle for survival. Against all odds, he beat the takeover, but Synergy Interstate had friends in high places. His success was undermined and ultimately defeated. Sinclair's skillful handling of the takeover challenge, turned heads at Synergy Interstate, and to their credit they brought him over as their new CEO. It was Sinclair who took, the then spent Synergy Interstate, and guided it to become the powerful, diversified, and international Synergy Earth. At the center of it all was an android species named eSly; the little "e" stood for his on-board flash memory.

But none of this mattered anymore.

- - - - ◇ - - - -

Tamura knew he was fighter pilot ace of the entire the Air Force. His orders were clear-cut: *Shoot the bogie down, period.* He was on the near-side, intercept course and *Wraith Two* would come up on the far side. The angle between *Wraith One and Two* would be 90 degrees and closing, by the time the alien aircraft flew past them. Tamura gazed, fighting back awestruck, as the alien airship shot past him. He adjusted his helmet to fully connect with the brain wave interface, inside. He released the *stick*, did a power roll, and came up to altitude.

"Wraith Two, I have a visual on the bogie; I'm armed and locking on target. What's your status?"

"Coming up into position and packing."

"Wraith Two, I have a lock – firing . . . Missile one is launched."

"Confirmed Wraith One . . . He's doing an extreme bank to port but I have a lock. My first missile is launched."

"Roger Wraith Two, we have two Lash missiles running hot for his tailpipe . . . What's he doing? Are you seeing that tight loop back to starboard, Stuff?"

"Roger Wraith One. He's got to be pulling 15 G's at least."

"Roger Two, he's got to be grunting hard enough to fill his pants . . . My missile is whipping around behind him – Wraith Two, there's radio interference; my missile lock is broken. He should be heading right at you. I'll give you a shoot command so your fire will lead him."

"Roger One."

"Reacquiring lock . . . *Wraith Two the lock is on you.* Eject! Eject! EJECT!!"

Stuff Johnson ejected, a split second soon enough, to see his plane veer to the right and erupt into a ball of fire. He surfed the shock wave in his pilots' seat.

"This is Stennis, Wraith One, what's your status up there?"

"Johnson's clear; I see his 'chute. Bogie is now doing a tight bank to his left, with Wraith Two's first missile arcing on his tail. Alien is turning an incredibly tight radius. He's trying to break the missile lock so it reacquires on me. That's what he did to Wraith Two."

"What's your plan Tamura?"

"Two can play this game – I've got the armrest cover open, button depressed, and rigged for auto-eject." (Were Tamura to black out, he'd release the armrest button, and auto-eject.)

"Risky businesses, Tamura."

"So's leaving the Capitol unprotected, Commander – going into a tight barrel-roll – full throttle."

Tamura's plan was to spiral up from the roll, allowing the missile to reacquire on the enemy fighter. He inflated the bag-belt around his lower waist and strained, tightening his stomach muscles hard to keep adequate blood and oxygen pumping to his brain . . .

Tamura came to with a cold wind slapping him in the face, hanging upside-down in his ejected seat. *Wham!* The Slash missile blew his downrange plane to smithereens.

Tamura righted himself, opened his seat belt, and ejected from the seat, causing his parachute to open. The enemy fighter did a tight vertical turn, and headed back the way it came at high speed . . . The Air Force would regroup and have its' day.

"Sly *0xABDC* to Hive Air Main: Mission accomplished and vectoring back to base," the pilot said, giving his name in the base 16 numbering system – hexadecimal.

"Regain your wireless link at the designated co-ordinates and we'll fly you back from there. Will you need to refuel at mid-flight? – we need to recamo the airstrip entrance."

"Negative."

"Confirmed here; you will have transport from the flight line to your debriefing,"

The android was already writing his digital report, including close-up pictures of two, perplexed looking parachutists. "Roger Air Main, I have already regained my link."

"Your mission was adequate and we await your arrival, linked *iSly*."

# Chapter 2
## His Honor

"Is stuff getting through, Mr. Sinclair?" Dane asked.

"We lost a dump site last month. A wireless, Internet up-link got installed and that was the end of it – why, I don't know. The local GDP and two alternates are getting us by for now . . . Garbage trucks go in, filled with food and consumer goods, but they don't leave completely empty," Sinclair said.

"What were they thinking when they displaced Xanthra the magician?" Dane asked, "Now we recover stuff the 'droids have pitched, right under their noses at the dumps. Meanwhile, the android citizenry goes on buying food and consumables, just to fill more dumpsters with them."

"Balance, Joe. We can't have major economic dislocations, now, can we?" Sinclair had a calming tone and he let Dane get it off his chest.

"There's not much of an economy out here, Mr. Sinclair. Just economists."

"It thrives when a new load finds its way here . . . Hey Joe, put the word out: I'm looking for someone good on communications and distribution since our supply dumps are in such a state of flux," Sinclair said, sensing where Dane was heading.

"So you're not ready for extraction?" Dane asked, concerned that Sinclair needed out of the Greens.

"Not a chance, Joe. I've found a niche here." There was laughter in Sinclair's eyes and a glow of confidence. "I'm doing something useful and that makes me feel alive and vital; how could I give it up right now? I used to imagine doing things for others, giving something back. I thought all that mattered was making money and some of it could go to an impersonal charity. But I never felt like I do now, even when I was fighting the wars and making the big money. Now that's it's gone – out of my way – this opportunity has dropped in my lap. It gives me a new perspective – I'm even finding happiness. And my life is changing. I have no near, term plans to go back."

"OK."

*Wilson Sinclair was a rare individual – one who could fall right off the Fortune 500 CEO list, end up 'embracing a dung-hill' and make something out of it*, Dane thought.

"I hope you don't get distracted like the kid who was given a truckload of pony shit. He got all excited, grabbed a shovel, and dug wildly, looking for the pony he just knew had to be in there."

"Now Dane, you've used an unprofessional word."

"Funny thing about the origin of the word, *shit* – I looked it up on the Internet. It didn't start out as a bad word, because it didn't even start out as a word . . . Back in the age of steamships, bat and bird droppings – guano – was a valuable fertilizer. It was carried in the holds of ships. Unfortunately, if sea-water got in, the mixture would react, causing explosions that sank ships. The solution was to stow the material high in the hold, so sea-water couldn't get to it. *Ship High In Transit – S.H.I.T.* was the resulting harmless acronym."

"So you're going to give that whole explanation every time you use that word, for those of us who mistakenly see it as unprofessional?" Sinclair asked.

"Guess I'll have to get a little card printed up."

*Something special was happening with Sinclair. How would that change when things got better? If things got better,* Dane wondered.

Sinclair nodded at a remote yurt, "You're here to talk to His Honor Reged," he said, referring to a former Arbitrator of the Supreme Council of Humans and Robots. His Honor had been displaced ten days earlier – to this Greens site #1.

"That's one of the reasons," Dane said, "Net-news had him as only a junior arbitrator – just over a year on the Council."

"Yes, Dane . . . the screwy thing is, he's a robot. Go figure."

"Do you trust him?"

"No reason not to Joe, he's very well educated, he's been well groomed, he's balanced, and he's fair-minded."

"How well do you know him?"

"We've sat by firelight and talked for hours. He's got a grasp of corporate law, balanced with the public good. He's the genuine article, best I can tell, Joe. Brilliant man . . . um 'droid."

"Has he shown any interest in your distribution center – asked questions about it?"

"No."

"Does he talk about his displacement from the Council?"

"Never."

"Does he talk to anybody else?"

"No Joe – You think he's a plant? Think they'd use such a high profile asset for that; wouldn't that defeat its own purpose?" Sinclair said with exasperation. "We're sifting spies out all the time, Joe. – They tend to be too helpful. He's not on our radar. Go talk to him and see what you think . . . and Joe, stop back here on your way out, will you? I've got something you should see."

"Roger that."

- - - - ◇ - - - -

Joe Dane and Bluegrass passed a ragged group of displacees, on the path to the yurt – people who had been living comfortably in the recent past. They still looked healthy, but stressed. A former street person was their leader: Sinclair's protégée. The irony was that some, former homeless and street people had found themselves, and had become leaders in the Greens. New displacees had a lot to learn: shelter, fire, water, edible plants, mushrooms, how to snare game, how to trap birds in a ditch, how to kill nutria, rats, and even how to bring down larger game.

"Once they get past eating termites and grubs, they're well on their way," according to Sinclair. The new "volunteers" were kept busy learning survival skills: how to keep from getting lost, staying warm, getting drinking water, and tracking. Then they'd specialize by skill: browsing, hunting, weapons, water and cooking, construction, leadership – even basket-weaving. An able team with cultivating and gardening skills was working hard to get the group more self-sufficient with food.

They neared the yurt. His Honor Reged sat on a plain, wooden chair in the entrance. He was professionally dressed, in spite of his recent disgrace. The Arbitrator motioned for them to be seated on a wooden bench to his right. They sat down, made introductions, and exchanged pleasantries.

"May the discombobulate day of my birth be cursed and stricken from the days of the year," the Arbitrator said with a wry smile.

"Your Honor?" Dane asked.

"I couldn't say things like that before. As an android I gain no pleasure from it, other than I have a new freedom of expression. *Hot double demurring.* Are you gentlemen offended by occasional expletives?"

"No sir," Dane said, "We salute your new freedoms and choices."

"Well said! You gentlemen are welcome professionals . . . Why are we meeting today?"

Dane came right to the point: He asked the Arbitrator about the cause of his displacement to the Greens.

"No, Mr. Dane," the Arbitrator said, shaking his head, "I cannot discuss privileged Council business."

"Of course Mr. Arbitrator . . . may I ask this: What was the official reason given for your expulsion from the Supreme Council?"

"The official reason was made public, was it not?"

"Yes, Your Honor but it was cryptic," Dane said respectfully. He also wanted to hear the reason expressed in His Honor's own words.

"The official reason given, was called virtual referencing, gentlemen. If you know what that is, then it's not cryptic."

Both Dane and Bluegrass paused, thinking of what virtual referencing might mean. Finally Dane spoke, "Thank you, Mr.

Arbitrator. Is there anything we can do for you? And may we continue this discussion at a later time?"

"Gentlemen, it is enough that our meeting has been significant. As an android I also take note that your tone has been respectful. It is possible we will meet again . . . You must be *bold*, and very courageous once you find yourselves in the Redux."

"Excuse me, Your Honor."

"I bid you both farewell. Good night and good luck."

"Thank you Mr. Arbitrator." Dane said. They rose, shook hands and departed. Dane and Adams trod the return path to Sinclair's lean-to.

"Bluegrass?"

"Yeah. Nice, weird gentleman."

"The 'cussing'?"

"Irrelevant. Something more significant: He's either got a busted program or he's telegraphing something, with the garbled Old Testament quotations, and sign-off from an ancient television newscast."

"Hold those thoughts, Bluegrass. If he's hinting at a big clue, we need to figure it out on the trip back. Did you see, though, Bluegrass, he included you, seeming to think you're ready for big, future events."

- - - - ◇ - - - -

Dane and Adams returned to the hand-out hovel. Sinclair was on his knees, operating a cute toy for three little toddlers. The scene was tender.

"That was quick," Sinclair said, rising and handing the toy off to the kids.

"The Arbitrator cut right to it."

"He doesn't beat around the bush; he's got a brilliant legal mind – and he's the quintessential professional," Sinclair said, dusting off his hands.

"Have you heard him use expletives before?"

Sinclair laughed, "He's cussing?"

"Lamely. He revels in his new freedoms . . . Has he ever quoted from the Bible or old television before?" Dane asked.

"Uh? Something new there. What happened?"

"It was all in riddles. We'll sort it out and maybe we can discuss it later . . . What's on your mind, Mr. Sinclair?"

"Yes Joe, come over here, I want you to see something." Sinclair walked to a side table and pulled a folded sheet off, from a piece of android anatomy. Damaged. "What do you make of this?" he asked.

"Android, right hip plate," Dane said. "Looks like it took a clean laser burn; hard to tell."

"Tell what?" Sinclair asked, raising his bifocals back on his hair.

"Well, early eSly had a communications port in this part of his anatomy – right in that burned area. Where'd you get this?"

"Local landfill, Joe. They've been turning up," Sinclair said, "eSly . . . that stands for electric . . ."

"Electro-Silicon Logic Array," Dane said . . . "Unusual find here, Mr. Sinclair. New developments, like this, can be significant . . . any change in android anatomy or culture, no matter how small. Please keep us informed."

Dane set the hip plate down, and Sinclair threw the sheet back over it.

eSly was the first android release. His initial cost and time-lines soared beyond original budgets – but recently the fully integrated, android population was paying big dividends, according to what the experts were saying. The world economy was actually good, on balance, steering a safe course between fiscal contraction and self-destruction. No more financial disasters, or boom and bust from peak oil. A fairer distribution of wealth existed worldwide, and responsibility was shared in maintaining infrastructure. No shortages of skilled professionals. Androids were living and working across the broad, cross-section of society – from government and business, to laborers, expatriates, and vagabonds. Some were in service jobs, health care, and media work. Others were homeless.

The eSly prototype lacked computing power and was weak and doddering, physically. He progressed to a more powerful and intelligent android: A breakthrough in hydrogen cell electricity, coupled with wireless, power transmission, produced large working currents, making for a 'droid that was stronger than most humans. Advances in computer power and programming held the promise of a more sophisticated result. eSly was a more intuitive 'droid now, and he was looking so much more human, many people had trouble seeing the differences.

Every android, like a home computer, had a unique IP address, could be tracked, and was slated for inclusion in group supervision. SlyMap was being created as an arm of the Supreme Council of Humans and

Robots to get every android tracked. It was vital the Council take on this needed function. All android physical changes and programming revisions, required Council evaluation and approval before release.

All of this was irrelevant too.

The conversation continued: "Dane, you don't know this, but I've followed your career," Sinclair said, his expression now one of a powerful executive, making a money decision.

"Your computer science and robotics skills were top-notch, but you cast them aside and dropped out of sight, surviving a blacklisting after the eSly takeover. You've retrained and now, uncommon works for the public good stem from your work on Demographics projects. Dane, I'd like to see you in our survival work here, but I sense there's rhyme and reason to why you're not. You are positioned for the end game. You're standing in the portal where worlds are in collision."

"Nothing like that Mr. Sinclair," Dane's said, taken aback and his face hinting a shade of pink. "Thanks, but good breaks have helped; that's all." Dane spoke as if he were unaware of the epic crisis lying ahead: Destiny vs. disaster in the balance. Denial can be good for the short term.

"Dane, I think your young assistant has it in him to be a player in this league."

Bluegrass nodded, accidentally.

"Funny thing, the Arbitrator seemed to be hinting at the same idea. Bluegrass has great talent but he won't let himself believe he's doing anything," Dane said.

They exited the lean-to, Sinclair clapping his hand on Dane's shoulder, "Joe stay heads up, keep positive – the answer will shake out . . . And do you mind looking in on Wheldan? He's in that pup-tent over by your car. We're trying to get him involved; I worry about him."

"Can do, Mr. Sinclair . . . thanks and take care."

"Goodbye, Joe and Bluegrass; nice meeting you Bluegrass. Drive safely." Wilson Sinclair, former, powerful CEO, waved a warm good-bye.

- - - - ◇ - - - -

They knocked on a tent pole of the sad, little hovel.

"Enter!" came the command from inside.

They opened the tent flap. A withered, old man sat on a cardboard box, busting apart with old magazines and newspapers.

"Do I know you?" he asked.

"We've met, sir – a long time ago," Dane said.

"Anyway, not now. Not now!" Ryan Wheldan, former World Robotics Finance Chairman ordered, waving them off. "See my secretary for an appointment. My time is valuable." He nodded at a parrot, huddled in a cage across the tent, missing most of her feathers. Wheldan sat there on his magazines, superciliously nibbling on a rat's head.

It was time to leave.

Dane and Bluegrass drove back in silence. An hour later they engaged the highway magstripe and rode it back to the office. The radio news was ablaze with reports about the aerial dog-fight on the East Coast.

# Chapter 3
## TatarKhan

The Department of Demographic Services was in eclipse. The third story, suite of offices was as disheveled as it was disfunctional: Stacks of old files lay on tables along aisles, stray pages littered the carpet. The office was still reeling from the series of blockbusters that had pounded home, striking at its' very reason for being.

The world was on a whole new chapter of history, now.

This morning, though, the office was buzzing about the incredible dog-fight staged near the nation's Capitol, the day before. Its blow to Air Force morale was clear, but the dog-fight's timing and overall motive were unclear and unsettling.

Dane sat at his desk deliberating, rolling a pencil between his hands. Upping the ante with this explosive confrontation seemed . . . irrational. So much had been done on the fringes and out-of-sight, up 'til now. This singular event did have maximum impact, for sure. Hopefully it would be an isolated event . . . Strangeness. Ready now, he turned to his computer, composed and sent an e-mail. His computer manner was casual but he got results – fast.

"You, using a computer, Dane. Things must be serious." It was Laura Rollins, Junior Analyst.

"People are complex beings, Laura. The computer is just a tool," Dane said with a twinkle in his eye.

"That's rip sure. I wish you were still teaching our computer classes . . . Dane, what's going on with the Greens. And how soon will the rest of us be huddled out there?"

"Oh, we can't let that happen, Laura; they'll have to get past Bluegrass and me first."

"Give me a break, Dane! What's Bluegrass going to do; jam the enemy servers with his body?"

"Servers – supercomputers – run networks, like the Internet, Laura; how could you jam enough of them, with one body, to seriously reduce bandwidth?"

"Bandwidth, Dane?"

"Data capacity, Laura. Remember the analogy of the big water pipe that gets its diameter constricted, so water flow is restricted? So less bandwidth . . . "

"Restricts data flow – yes, and you had me believing there was a byte bucket for leaks."

Before Dane could answer, Hillary Smith, the Office Manager appeared.

"Mr. Dane, the Director needs your field report before 3 PM."

Hillary was efficient and very proper. She was the professionally, disgraced daughter of an US Senator. She was educated at Vassar and had been a key member of her father's staff. Her future seemed blue sky unlimited, but the Senator's career came to hinge on the watershed issue, of the safe and sane use of androids in society. It got done right, but by a shrewd technicality that forced the outcome. An investigation revealed it had originated in Hillary's section – and the political tide was going the wrong way at the time. She took the fall over it and her father was devastated. But Hillary never looked back, never complained. Seeing the android issue get done right, seemed to be enough: Hillary's political legacy. She was always professionally dressed, and she was an accomplisher, though she was of just average size and height. Dane always showed respect and patience towards her.

"She'll have it, Hillary," Dane said in a positive tone.

"That will be adequate," Hillary said, turning to stride, smartly, toward the Survey Section.

"That will be adequate," Laura mimicked, using a nasal twang, "That dame's got to be a robot with a defective people skills routine."

Dane gulped hard, but couldn't completely hide a smile.

"So. . .TatarKhan, Internet/ Hypernet Master. Is he on your caseload now?" Laura asked, looking at Dane's computer monitor.

"No, but it could end up the other way around. . .gotta go now; later Laura," Dane said, heading for the break room.

He bought a pint of milk and a chocolate brownie from the vending machine.

Samuel Cooke, Ops Manager, walked in and sat down next to him.

"Chocolate brownie – was the trip to the Greens all that rough, Joe?"

Dane smiled, relaxing, as they talked about his trip.

"Population density is going critical in the Greens, Sam."

"Higher class of human bean out there too, now, Dane."

"Yes. But I didn't exactly say it that way in my report."

"Will read it with interest . . . I got a call yesterday, Dane. It was security encrypted and from high places I can't disclose, but it was high places above the stratosphere."

"OK." There was little doubt in Dane's mind as to the executive office where the call had originated. "Was it about that crazy dogfight in Capitol air-space, yesterday?"

"Yes, and the whole Beltway's ringing with aftershocks. They don't know what to tell Congress about it. They don't know what to tell the press about it, let alone the people. Because there's major, public unrest over it, at all levels, they're feeling enormous pressure to do something, but they don't know what to do – not a clue. And I was hearing and being asked all kinds of things."

"I can imagine," Dane said.

"Some Senators want the military to take over and get Sigma Force, which we know doesn't exist, involved. It's hard to blame them, knowing the pressure they're under from their constituents. Our special operators are phenomenal at hostage rescues, getting on airplanes through middle escape hatches and sweeping to both ends. Picking, opening, or blasting their way through any door in the world, to an objective, is child's play to them. I'd happily let them take over, but the leaders realize they're at a loss as to which door, in the whole world, they'd tell them to attack. They can't just blow up some 'droid think tank and dust off their hands; the public would see right through it. Besides, there would be big legal issues about an operation within our borders."

"Long story and three-ring circus short, it's right back in our laps, Dane. We discussed helping our CT, counter-terrorist forces, to start boning up on robotic science and the core, cyberDNA kernel of eSly, but that would take too long and nobody would buy it anyway. So it has to turn out that our top people and operatives are on it like blood hounds, 'til the bad 'droids are caught and brought to justice – something like that."

"How long did this all take?" Dane asked.

"Plenty long," Sam said with a mirthful grin. "Dane, I'm not telling you all this so you feel pressured, or get distracted. Pressure smessure, we're working hard on it, what else can we do? Getting this Hypernet master on, if he's as good as we hope, should make a difference. They know his background in non-existent Sigma Forces, even if we don't. That will make them think one of their own is right in on the front line. I don't know how our new guy will think about it, though. What I'm getting is, he's kind of a free spirit."

"Otherwise things are kind of dull and normal around here, and we're a long ways away from where they ain't"

"Dane chuckled in relief."

Sam Cooke was a good head. This dim era was lucky to have him. He was always the well-groomed professional – pleasant, infectiously positive, and he was able to poke fun at reversals in fortune, cutting them down-to-size. He somehow did his work with an immunity to the flood of negative news. A good trait because recent events had been a spate of negativity. He had the knack of dropping an irreverent twist of humor about something bad, that was going down, making it look ridiculous. Maybe that was how he kept his objectivity.

Only halfway through his brownie, Dane's wearable computer signaled e-mail. He pulled it out from his inside coat pocket, where he'd stuffed it. He glanced at a cryptic response to his recent e-mail:

> "Not much we see, these days, is rad;
> the odds are on the hot-wired fad.
> > TatarKhan

> "North Shore Drive, past the Ship's Lantern
> Pub; 'bout two hours before sunset. Drive south
> 'til your e-mail texts you 'TK'.

O.K.?"

"E-mail from guess who. Excuse me, Mr. Sam. May I call you in a few minutes?" Dane asked.

"Sure Joe . . . I don't expect you got much out of His Honor, Reged."

"Hard to say, Sam; need your analysis on our report."

Dane went to his desk, sat down and thought a minute, then e-mailed the following:

"TK;
Yes. Go!
Dane.

Ps. Car is a blue runner, Electro-Blade series."

Then he grabbed his phone. Hit Sam's extension. "Sam, I've got to leave now on company, hypernet business. Can Blue boy fill in our report outline, and run it by you, on its way to the Director? See how the weirdness strikes you?"

"Works for me, Joe. All is benign up here," Sam replied, understanding where Dane was heading. "But don't get too far a-field before this report gets digested. We need to invent an adequate cover for you and Bluegrass."

"Understand, Sam. I'll tell Bluegrass. Thanks."

Any absence from the daily fallout from the Shift event was welcome; it hung over everything like a cloud of gloom. The upshot of the Shift was 'droid self-replication: the design and building of super-androids, by androids. Using the latest technology.

The Shift was inexplicable and it set whole nations on the slippery slope, sliding towards their worst fear – catastrophe. Major dislocations had come with the Shift: the creation of the Greens, for one. Professional roboticists were mystified by the sinister trend, because robot programming had always been open-source. Revisions were submitted worldwide, over the Internet, to the Council of Humans and Robots, for study, modification, rejection, or approval. Every shred of programming code had always been sifted, exhaustively, by the Council, before-and-after being released. But the code that drove the shifted androids was out-of-reach for the Council, or for any known person.

One question loomed over all others: Was some major player – mastermind, villain, or rogue android – crafting and guiding this ominous turn of events? It was Dane's job to unravel the mystery, quickly. How many months or years of a head start did it have on him? Unknown. It was like coming into a movie that was half over; now, catch the story line, name the major players, and solve the mystery before it ended.

Dane had no official cover; he wasn't DCI, Department of Central Intelligence. He was in no-man's-land, vulnerable and in danger, but that was everybody now. His orders were verbal, coming from high places. Dane finessed his regular demographic projects, but his scope and focus had become the unraveling this 'droid enigma. He submitted regular reports. Someone in high office was taking soundings of what got stirred up, he realized. It was good that Sam Cooke knew about all this and was handling it.

Dane was on the ground with advanced, inside knowledge that made him, unique. A superb counterterrorist force was surely on alert, but there was no time for them to ascend the steep learning curve they'd need . . . Once when Dane and Sam Cooke were going over Tater-Khan's resume, Sam first dropped the comment, "Dane, Sigma Force doesn't exist; there's no such CT team." *With TaterKhan aboard, things should be good at that end,* Dane realized. At least Dane had Sam Cooke as his back, shielding him so he could work. Now Sam was creating his cover that would include an obscure Hypernet Master.

Dane cruised along North Shore Drive, running on-time. His Electro-Blade made a pleasant hum as it followed the magstripe, implanted in the lane. It was a clear, sunny afternoon, not unusual for this time of year and not cold. The sunlight glinted brightly from the waves and reflected off the road. Dane was wearing his polarized sunglasses. And the drive was enjoyable. Pleasant memories played at the edges of his mind: When he and Belyn were younger, they'd pack up food, hibachi, rent a cut-rate beach cabin, and stay the weekend. They always brought a pet: a kitten, a puppy – a bird in a cage once . . . great memories but duty called.

He approached a viewpoint over a deserted part of the beach. *I've got a hunch about this place,* Dane thought. *bBeep.* It was his on-person computer, a headband unit with a small monitor off to the right. Voice activated.

"Yes," Dane answered.

The message *TK* appeared.

Dane drove into the viewpoint; parked and locked the vehicle. The lookout was called Survivor's Beach and it was 3:07 PM. There was a stone stairway, at an opening in the stone wall, surrounding the turnout. The opening led to a path, down through the beach grass. *Survivor works,* Dane thought, heading for the opening. It was fine, stone masonry. An old, weathered text was sculpted on the right side, reading: "Enter here survivor. You who would save man from strange machinations." *Eeriness.*

A light breeze streamed through the beach grass. Plover birds stirred here and there and seagulls worked the ebbing tide. Childhood memories flashed into Joe's mind as he walked down the path, the sand filling his shoes.

"Look, here's a sand dollar," Diane his older sister had said. The thought of money to be made had crossed his young mind . . . *Deep sea fishing, crabbing, clam-digging, and livin' in a beach cabin. It was all so safe. How did the good life get so fouled up?*

The path descended toward the beach, and soon Dane was down on it. A bearded figure, of average height and size, appeared at Dane's side. He'd been waiting in an area where the beach sand bayed into the grassy layer. His eyes were bright – intelligent – and he radiated a disarmingly, sincere personality: so different from his e-mails.

"TatarKhan?" Dane asked.

"Yes, Joe Dane." TatarKhan said, as he scanned him with a hand-held object, "Hey man. You're human!"

"Very," Dane said, curious about what was happening.

"Ancient transistor radio," TatarKhan said, "Androids still give off an electric signature; the radio picks it up as static."

Dane nodded. . . "Survivor's Beach and an e-mail written in old slang, TatarKhan?"

"Walk with me along the Beach, Dane. We'll have 20 minutes of complete privacy . . . "

"Yeah, the ancient slang, it gets missed by SpyNet. Don't be surprised if my next e-mail is written in Shakespearian English."

The two of them walked north, conversing as the surf rolled. *If nothing comes of this, it's a great day for the beach,* Dane thought. It was sunny, warm, and the tide was out. Seagulls fought over a treasure, one of them had found, by charred logs from an extinguished beach fire. The aroma of salty seaweed and kelp filled his nostrils as they passed an intensely, green mass of it, washed up with a piece of driftwood already dry in the sun. Dane could taste salt on his lips and the aroma of an abandoned pier nearby was light on the air. Only a cargo carrying hover-craft plied the ocean – far out.

"You're a gifted artist, TatarKhan, if your website was right in crediting you as the artist of the beautiful and powerful art display there."

"Oh, I've always loved art, Dane. That was my true motive in starting with computers."

"That's starting to make sense to me . . . There's an underlying force, a direction to your art. Lots of color woven in, great backgrounds, great perspective, and very thematic, but with a simplicity and sincerity of purpose. But it's held back enough so it doesn't compete too much with the text message on the site, which I almost forgot to read while studying the art. I think I've seen that accomplished style before, somewhere, but under a different name. Did you take fine art courses in your college career?" Dane was happy this subject was close to TaterKhan's heart.

"I did as many as I could and I have an unlisted minor in art. My art has been displayed back east, but under a pseudonym. At present, I can't be both artist and Hypernet master – too many complications with my official background. So I do the art under the artist name – no it's not ArtarKhan. I turn out two or three pieces a year, but have to remain somewhat of a mystery man to my public. I've done a very few interviews and appearances – I'll be able to do more later on after I graduate, maybe from this present fiasco."

"Are you thinking about the recent air battle, involving Air Force aces, TaterKhan?"

"I think about it as little as possible, Dane, since I can't do a thing about it at their end."

"That about sums up how I feel about it. We're seeing a lot more stuff happening closer to home, in android land and on the Internet. Hopefully we can do something about that."

"The Internet's turned radical, Dane. It's all since that stinking android Shift," TatarKhan said, "There's a void now – a big black hole in the Internet. Web-servers and bandwidth are falling right into it. Dropping clear out of sight. You're here because society's voiding out too. Isn't that true, Dane?" TatarKhan's expression showed open concern.

"Maybe," Dane said.

TatarKhan had come to the Internet young, a free spirit, and full of piss and vinegar. His youthful irreverence had been exceeded only by his personality and creativity. He came up through Naval Intelligence, and was already turning heads by the time he started aceing classes in top academies. His willingness to teach and to help others, landed him a stint as Section Chief of Computer Intelligence and Security – Black Ops – in the Office of National Security. Dane had this information and the answers to most of his questions. He needed to hear TatarKhan's take on the issues, though.

*Their meeting on short notice, his sincerity, and the graying at his temples, indicate a maturity in TatarKhan,* Dane thought. *He realizes serious changes are going down in life, and on the Internet. I'm talking to an able, serious mover in his prime.*

"What's your real name, TatarKhan?"

"Just call me Pete or Tark, if you want. TatarKhan's my Internet name . . . Yeah, it sounded cool when I took it 25 years ago. TartarKhan would've been better, but my friends only knew fish and tartar sauce."

"But not the Tartars of ancient history . . . You have an impressive resume," Dane said, "Though who you are may be known to me already."

"Oh, yeah. . .apart from a gap in my Naval resume, I can't talk about. I've programmed on the web using everything from XHTML and Apache Web Server, to C++ and PHP. You need encryption; I've got it. If you need invisibility, I have Hypernet. Here's my card, Mr. Dunn some big things too." TatarKhan had regained his irreverent bounce.

Dane looked at the card. It read *TatarKhan! Internet/ Hypernet Master.* The dot below the exclamation point was embossed.

"Some of the old, web programming software, you named, goes way back," Dane said.

"Ah . . . " TatarKhan said, breathing deeply, "Those were the good, cgi, code writing days, Dane. Internet's too easy now—boring. Hypernet has brought back the joy: all kinds of new and clever toys."

"Pete, about this android Shift. More went down than just the announced eSly upgrade; true?"

"A lot more Dane: First came the RoboLinux download, ROX, a breakthrough, android operating system. Next came the neural net, a pyramid of software objects and routines, including chaos-handling tools. The *Shift* compiled them in eSly; the coding was so subtle, it created a human-like intelligence and personality most people can't see through. The ROX Operating System was supposed to be open source – but it is *not*. Inscrutable it is, *yes*."

"What about the source code that Robolinux is compiled from?"

"You're getting at the *core* issue here, Dane. I think when the code is first downloaded in a 'droid, you can get at it, read it, understand and copy it. It should be stored in android memory, as just text code. The android is still eSly and the code is vulnerable at this stage. We can dig through it to our heart's content. When the *Shift* is induced, the files self-extract, compile, and overwrite the eSly persona. As you know, compiled code is just ones and zeroes and most of the information, we'd recognize, is stripped away."

"The android becomes something different, and it involves the

Internet. It's probably called something like IntSly. Or iSly," TatarKhan said, "The iSly androids who're heisting the Internet."

"And taking over the world . . . IntSly, iSly; you mean Internet SiliLogic Array?"

"Yes. And sly you are to this Dane, double meaning intended. . . There are those obscure, web references to a bright, young roboticist named Dunn, central to the eSly breakthroughs. Lassen and Dunn, connecting the dots found by the great robotic theorists. So androids got created, learned, and committed new knowledge to flash memory; flash being the 'e' as in eSly. But now it's the little letter 'i' is for Internet, in iSly. And a huge diversion of Internet resources, Dane."

"Forget about dim antiquity and the shadows of mere coincidence: The robotocist, Dunn, you just spoke of was dreamed up, dreamed about, and dreamed away . . . About that core issue, Pete."

TatarKhan whipped out a global positioning unit and pointed at a trace on a map. "This is a Bureau of Land Management android, out doing a topographical survey," TatarKhan said intently, "He's been out in the sticks since summer, so he's sure to have the downloads, but no *Shift* for him yet. He has to come within range of wireless Internet or another iSly, for the *Shift* to be induced, which would lock us out."

Dane nodded, *This explains the loss of the dump sites that went wireless,* he thought. "Yeah, Tark, I've seen this at work. And the Shift comes in scheduled stages?"

"Do you think because robots are doing the programming, it doesn't take stages and revisions, Dane? Just like with humans, it takes time for an android to build a good cyber-mechanical creation; just like with humans it takes time to get all the bugs out. You've been through all this. How could a 'droid just snap his fingers and have the finished product – no testing, editing, or developing? . . . But this buys us some time."

Dane nodded.

"Anyway, this BLM guy's scheduled to show up, right here, on High Pass Road next weekend," TatarKhan said, pointing at a red star on his GPS display. "From there he'll probably hike to Burnt Woods, you know, the Ranger Station. From there, he'll get a ride; only the ride should be with us." TatarKhan had his web-master hat on now.

"Unusual situation, nice work," Dane said, "What else can you tell me about him?"

"What do you need, Dane? Name, address, Universal I.D number?"

Dane thought for a full minute. . ."Tark, can you pull up a chart on him?"

"What kind of chart? You mean a medical char. . .t" TatarKhan broke off in mid-sentence, eyes squinting down the beach. Faint shadows came into focus as two erect, well dressed figures, striding in their direction.

*Perfect 'droid profile, or two Marine D.I.s out on a stroll*, Dane thought.

"It's getting late Tark," Dane said, "Need a ride back to town? We can talk more and discuss your fee."

"Yeah, it's time. Let's go *now!*," TatarKhan said.

- - - - ◇ - - - -

They drove south, away from the action, then took an alternate route back to SF North.

After the great rift earthquake of 2053 leveled San Francisco and everything up the coast, Coos Bay and its new, geologic long island, thrived to become a fresh and unexpected urban center on the West Coast – at the cost of the leveling of a major urban area, the fault-line displacement of a chunk of the northern California coast, and a huge migration of refugees who fled inland, given early warning by animal behavior.

"What's causing this 'droid-Internet crisis Dane; do you know?" TatarKhan's sincerity was surprising. Web-savant or not, he knew this was serious stuff.

"I do not, Pete. I just have a broader, more sinister take on the symptoms. We know it began when eSly started fabricating iSly. Like you said, iSly rocked a seismic cyber-wave worldwide, but what caused his emergence is unknown. iSly is an inexplicably, spontaneous, super-eSly. With iSly replicating himself, super-androids are appearing at a slow but exponential rate—picking up steam now. They comprise a whole new group of people in society – including jet fighter pilots. – Some demographic! And they're aloof, Pete; they march to their own drumbeat, and they've become outright hostile. Our leaders are terrified of where they could be taking us."

"Isn't there a mover behind this, someone plotting this, like shadowy figures in government or industry?"

"Pete, the high and mighty of every sector in society are getting bumped to places, collectively called the Greens. Along with a lot of common millionaires and everyday people like you and me. No one in power seems to be doing this."

"Loose cannon then, just a rogue process, no one's behind it?" TatarKhan asked.

"We need to find out, Tark . . . Is there a sinister personality in high places nursing this along – king of moles? That can't be ruled out, either . . . Working together, I know we can bust this case."

# Chapter 4
## Medical Exam

"**W**here's the admin? Call the admin," cried the head orderly. He was an android, standing at the rear door of the clinic. Bluegrass had parked the ambulance across two reserved spaces, and the orderly went after him.

Dane and TatarKhan dutifully wheeled in a patient, strapped to a gurney, through the entrance vacated by the orderly. The patient was wearing blue jeans and a flannel shirt. The gurney disappeared down the hallway and the door swung shut.

"Thanks Blue, see you Monday," Dane toned into his headset speaker.

"OK, Dane. I'm gone, and with luck, I'll get this nut to chase me down the street."

"Have fun Blue," Dane said, "but remember he's just a 'droid." He switched the audio off and stuffed the headset back inside his orderly smock.

"Shinola-fire! Dane this is Ward D, the cuckoo's nest," TatarKhan whispered.

"No worries Pete; lobotomies done only on holidays. Third door on the left."

A nurse smiled, standing by, as they wheeled the gurney into Dr. William's clinic. "This is the android *EBEC*?" she asked. EBEC was the name number of the android, in the hexadecimal, numbering system. (Hexadecimal digits are 0 -15.)

"Yes nurse; here's his medical card," Dane said, handing it over.

"And you suspect he was injured, or damaged, while doing a topographical survey?" she asked with concern.

"Yes nurse, he's with the Interior Department."

"I see. Please wait here in D-3," she said, guiding them in, "The Doctor will see you soon."

They handed her the patient's boots, in a lead-lined bag.

"And you want these checked for radiation contamination?" the nurse asked.

Dane nodded.

Another smile and she was gone.

The room looked and smelled like a medical exam room: exam table, sphygmomanometer, scopes, bio-hazard container, instruments, other labeled containers, and magazines askew in a rack next to a chair. A flat paneled PC computer sat on a side desk. A coil of advanced, networking cable was connected to the computer.

"Tark, sit him up on the exam table, will you?"

"You heard the man, EBEC," TatarKhan said to the 'droid, "Kindly get up and sit on this table – let your legs hang over the end."

The android sat up and got onto the paper-covered exam table. His movements were lithe, accompanied with a soft whirring of servo motors. TatarKhan shoved the gurney to the side.

"Master TatarKhan, my Cyclical Redundancy Check diagnostic, senses neither memory loss nor corruption," EBEC said, trying to be helpful.

"Ah, this Order of Diagnostic is to rule out more systemic, radiation damage to your computer system, bud." TatarKhan assured him.

"Certainly, Sir," the 'droid said, "Please let me know if I can be helpful in any way."

TatarKhan rolled his eyes and nodded.

Soon a graying physician entered the room. He was white smocked, white bearded, and white mustachioed – impeccably groomed. "Patient's hex name is 0xEBEC: What's your Internet IP address, EBEC?" the Doctor asked, picking up the network cable.

"Here Dane, have your man plug him in, will you?" Dr. Williams sat down at the computer and keyed the numbers and dots into an Internet browser, as EBEC recited them. "Do I have a link light blinking on the 'droid?" the Doctor asked.

TatarKhan nodded and said, "Clear channel expressly to Gilead of Tropics White."

The Doctor hit *Enter* on the keyboard. "And who is this?" he asked, ignoring the comment.

"Dr. Williams, meet TatarKhan, Net HyperMaster," Dane said, grimacing at TatarKhan. Dane had taken courses with Dr. Williams when he did under-graduate work in cybernetics.

"Nice meeting you, TatarKhan. Your high intelligence is not hidden by your irreverent style."

"Thank you, Dr. Williams."

Dane smiled.

The computer screen blinked and a web page formed. "What! *iSly?*" the Doctor shouted, rising, "This is new, Dane; get your savant in front of this. Take this chair, right here, TatarKhan."

TatarKhan pulled an external memory stick from his bag, and took the Doctor's chair. "May I make a copy?" he asked.

"The LightSpeed port's on the left side, TatarKhan – knock yourself out."

TatarKhan attached the memory stick to the computer and started searching the spartan web page. "Communications, neural net drivers . . . " TatarKhan mumbled to himself, as he searched the web page, embedded in the 'droid. EBEC sat eye's closed: He was in rest mode. "Kernel! Wait a minute . . . Yes! Robolinux source code," TatarKhan said, smiling like a kid who'd just gotten a new cell phone.

"Anything in English? Comments?" Dane asked, looking over TatarKhan's shoulder.

"Sparse; most of it's just code headings," TatarKhan said, initiating the download of the code.

WHAM – Crash!! Suddenly, the room jolted and shook crazily! Ceiling tiles and instruments went flying. "Whoa!" TatarKhan yelled, as he grabbed the downloading PC. He rode his chair, like a cowboy riding a bronc. Dane and the Doctor steadied EBEC.

A nurse burst into the room. "Doctor, a speeding fire truck has struck the building!" she cried. Suddenly the android started a rapid, random blinking; he shuddered and shook, within Dane's grasp.

"Is the building in danger of collapsing?" the Doctor yelled.

"No," said the nurse. LED lights flashed on her waist-worn computer. She stood so that her wireless port pointed directly at EBEC, unnoticed in the confusion.

"Get Admin and Triage on it, nurse," the Doctor said.

The nurse stared clinically at EBEC. She was short and ordinary, but she had an intense focus – 'droid like.

"Now, nurse!" the Doctor barked.

The nurse looked down at her display, pressed a button, turned and marched out.

"Who was that, Jeff?" Dane asked. (They were on a first name basis since taking classes together.)

"Never laid eyes on her before," answered the Doctor. He took a deep breath and slumped down on the waiting chair. Waved an OK.

"What've you got, Pete?" Dane asked.

TatarKhan shook his head and pointed at a pop-up window on the monitor. It read:

> There will be no response from http://wrw.isly.org/ – the server could be down or is not responding. If you are unable to connect again, contact the server's administrator.

"Android Shift, right under our noses. And it is *iSly*, using something called the Worldwide Robotic Web," TatarKhan said, detaching his equipment and stuffing it back in his bag. He was agitated. "That beady-eyed, bitch, gynoid nurse shifted him."

"Gynoid as in female android . . . Where did she come from?" Dane asked . . . defining gynoid. Hope does not throw something off.

"RN parallel-universe hell, for all I know, Joe. I've got to get out to that wreck," the Doctor said.

"OK, Dr. Williams. Thanks." he answered in a subdued tone.

"Your patient's in order otherwise, Dunn; I'll e-mail the paperwork to your office. We have to give priority to what's critical now. Just don't tell me where you got that crazy ambulance."

"What a shame," Dane said, smiling.

The doctor grabbed his medical bag and hurried out of the exam room.

"Nothing left for us here – let's fly, Pete! Just leave him be; he can sit, compile, and link to program libraries all day, if he wants," Dane said.

TatarKhan cleared the monitor and detached EBEC from the network cable.

The android sat fibrillating on the exam table. TatarKhan closed the door, locking it on their way out.

The front end of a huge, red fire truck sat where it had crashed into the clinic lobby. It was a nest of medical, triage activity. On Sundays only a reduced staff worked the lobby. A couple of damaged 'droids sat at the other end. Medics on site, and those arriving by the minute, had the scene covered.

Dane and TatarKhan stepped outside, through a broken, picture window frame in front. They went unnoticed in the confusion.

*KA-Wham!* The D-3, Exam room door flew off its hinges. An erect figure, wearing a flannel shirt and blue jeans, emerged. He crossed the lobby and began assisting the two injured androids.

"No more Master TatarKhans from your former, buddy EBEC," Dane said, subliminal to the noise inside. Unobserved they headed west on Wilshire Boulevard. It was a bright day. The sun was destined to set near the far center of the Boulevard. Sunday shoppers and street people were gathering. Sirens sounded in the distance. The two kept moving, walking north a block, and then slipping down a side street. The downtown was busy with shoppers, tourists, and a few professional people. The sirens sounded on Wilshire now.

"Did you get anything?" Dane asked.

"iSly it is; not much else, Joe. We suspected iSly means Internet Silicon Logic Array . . . there was something, Joe."

"Tark?"

"There was a reference to a template file called 'Archetype'; it was in the ethics declarations . . . and it had an ambiguous comment."

"What?" Dane asked.

TatarKhan pulled a notepad from his pocket. He'd scribbled out the code snippet in the exam room. "It's 'Class Arche type murrow.redux.istream(lov),'" he said, giving it to Dane, "Typical C++ programming language, text. Like it's calling a routine from somewhere outside of the 'droid's processor, or main memory, Joe."

"(Class Arche) type murrow . . . – that plays on the word *Archetype*. Anything else?" Dane asked, handing the notepad back to TatarKhan.

"I'll parse out the little I have. It's not much," TatarKhan said, still seeming hyper.

"The little we got may prove hot," Dane said.

They walked three more blocks in silence.

"Are you OK Pete?" Dane asked.

"I'm good – just a little buzzed from playing doctor in crazy-land," TatarKhan said. He looked steamed, though, like something was coming.

"Joe, we've been living in lameo-land, run by ideologue crackers," TatarKhan posited.

"What ideas, Pete?" Dane asked, drawing him out.

"Androids in the mix with people – our nursey norms. I've been thinking about this a long time: They helped us over some hurdles at the start, but that was enough. If we're too stinking lazy to take responsibility for our own successes and screw-ups, what good are we? How do we expect to get anywhere? The goodie 'droids helped the economy too, but things have gone too far. Now they're self-replicating, using the latest technology. Gaining the upper hand. Nurse is taking it all over and people, lulled to sleep, are in a bad way."

Dane listened while TatarKhan vented.

"I hear you," Dane replied, allowing Tark time to get it all out and cool off.

A space of silence . . .

"We're in a strange, risk corridor, Pete . . . about the code: Can you work out how the ROX operating system communicates over the Internet – how it encrypts?"

"Exactly Dane; I'll work on a data packet diagram – headers, data, tailers. Maybe we can have the enjoyment of hacking their servers."

- - - - ◇ - - - -


Integrating robots into the human population – the AndRan Project – was the grand experiment of the last quarter century. The plan was to create a class of android citizens, a stabilizing force in the world. *Bringing us a grand, new, prosperous future through influence and example*, was the happy-talk, sales pitch.

The real reason for AndRan was to prevent a human extinction event. Too many world climate dials had turned critical, too many weather patterns and changes had hit home. The loss of the Great Plains farm-belt to desert, for one, and the near loss of the Gulf Stream from giant glaciers, shed by Greenland, for another. The leaders and movers of the world came to realize that built-in, enforced changes had to come, in order to open a survival path for humanity. A whole, new, non-human world population had to be created to make this road to survival possible. Mainly through their example, good individual traits, but with enough political and economic clout to tip the scales in favor of living.

The android demographic, as it came to be called, had been a major project involving issues of geopolitics, anthropology, climatology, economics, sociology, international relations, sports, public opinion, conflict resolution, and myriad others. The androids were designed to live like humans: in homes and apartments, work at jobs, earn a living, save and invest money, and vote for "good" candidates in elections, but using a vastly, reduced carbon foot-print. They bought earth-friendly consumer items, and like humans: food, clothing, appliances, cars, even products for leisure time activities. They went on trips, they saw doctors and dentists, and they looked more like human beings as time went on, due in large part to plug-in prosthetics. Their entry into the world was seamless, supposedly, and it helped build an environmental economy – jobs were plentiful then. *The many hitches and bugs that have appeared are insignificant, compared to the better good*, people were told.

Of course the Project had its detractors – one faction was called the Grasslanders. They were suspicious of corporate-military interests. Their spokesman, Alan Seder, warned: "The American and world workforce is becoming debilitated, physically and mentally by agra-business food, is poorly educated, and is hypnotized by mass media. Multinational corporations only want skilled, tireless androids filling the workplace, replacing human workers. Working conditions will deteriorate. What could be better for the corporate giants than to have dull, predictable, android wage-earners, buying retail products, only to recycle them."

Major strikes and labor unrest came with the new android citizenry, until leaders decided that blue collar 'droids would become union members – *infiltrators* according to labor leaders. Surprising enough, though, the 'droids turned out to be moderately conservative; good labor contracts became the rule.

Dane and TatarKhan's focus was on matters demanding more immediate attention.

# Chapter 5
## Improv

They'd walked about a mile from Wilshire Medical Clinic, but the center of official activity was spreading. Uniformed officers on motorcycles, passed on cross streets and a helicopter was flying above, vectoring out a search pattern. They saw an android cop bolt from an alley a few blocks up, cross the street, and continue down the alley.

"Dane, they're scouring the place for us; think I saw a 'droid buzz across the street behind us, a minute ago. That hook-and-ladder stunt was too big a whoop, just to let it drop. They know we're onto something."

"Pete, they're looking for two male nurses . . . Hey, check out this western store."

They entered an old fashioned, western haberdashery and slipped down the second aisle. It was bigger than they expected and the clerks all seemed busy. Dane grabbed a black and red shirt with sequins, blue jeans, and a belt.

"Grab yer duds pard; it's on me," Dane said.

Ten minutes later they had on colorful shirts, jeans, belt-buckles, boots, and fancy Stetsons, waiting to pay at the front counter. Dane had wrapped up their medical smocks in paper stock from the back room.

"Morning, gents," the clerk greeted, as he scanned the price tags. "Here, use this sack for your street clothes."

Dane slipped the paper-wrapped bundle into the sack the clerk had handed him.

"Y'all headed for the country jam at the Flamingo Flush Corral?"

"Like a dogie to his mama, pard," Dane drawled, "Look at us, buying our country clothes, ready to go, but with no instruments."

"Yeah, lousy baggage handling; happens all the time," the clerk said, "Smitty's three doors up, just before the block ends; he's good on stringed instruments. Does that help?"

Dane nodded. "And the Corral?"

"Nine more blocks up from Smitty's; other side of the street. You'll see a country crowd."

Dane and TatarKhan found themselves walking toward Smitty's. "Do you play anything, Tark?"

"Banjo, Dane. What about you?"

"Had some violin lessons and I do jazz fiddle, nights, to relax."

They bought economy but good-sounding instruments at Smitty's, and headed on their way.

A delivery truck pulled up to the curb in front of them. The driver jumped out and ran across the street, into the high-rise there, carrying a package. Dane slipped into the van, walked down the aisle, and shoved the smock sack under the bottom shelf, behind the right, rear wheel-well. He got back on the sidewalk quick and continued walking with TatarKhan, who wore a smirk and was muttering something about earth-orbit delivery.

They saw the Flamingo Flush Corral, blocks away. A crowd stood outside of what looked like an old movie theater. They were all in western garb and many carried instrument cases. Dane and TatarKhan sauntered up and got in line.

Big action was close at hand: Two male nurses wearing medical smocks exited a restaurant across the street. A motorcycle policeman up the road spotted them. He was on his radio, and in seconds, police cars and motorcycles screamed up, braking to a stop by the nurses. Lights flashing. One police car fishtailed, knocking a motorcycle into another police car. Instantly the medicos were lying prone on the sidewalk. Officers snapped handcuffs on them, and guns were drawn. A police paddy-wagon approached, its sirens wailing. The western group rushed to the sidewalk, to see what was happening across the street. Dane and TatarKhan slid on up the line.

"Will you be professional or amateur?" the ticket lady asked them.

"Amateur Ma'am," Dane said with a smile, "You have a pretty smile, Ma'am."

"Oh, you cowboys," she said, embarrassed, "That'll be 50 e-units each."

Dane pulled out a generic, money card and she scanned it in.

"Box lunches are on the far counter; amateur music's just to the right. You start eating at 11:15 AM, then go on the stage when the professional group takes lunch at noon."

Dane and TatarKhan strode through the glass doors, not turning to look back. They headed for the food and grabbed their music books. The lobby was decorated and muraled out as a desolate grassland. A 16" high, hillock prop lay toward the front of the lobby. It was covered with dry grass and was garnished with wild flowers. Stepping stones allowed for travel across the flowered mound.

The main theater was a breathtaking, Saguaro cactus forest at sunrise. The mural art was big, colorful, and Arizonan. Massive, artificial cacti stood at the right, front corners of four of the six audience sections. The main stage extended out over the orchestra pit, below, and some booths – fenced pens – were set along either side wall. Most of them had small stages for music rehearsal. Dane and TatarKhan found seats on the front row. The excitement outside was dying down and the theater began to fill with the western group.

People were still buzzing about the scene outside. "It stinks to be in health care these days," said one little guy wearing thick, black glasses, and a red bandanna, "If you don't have the right connections, you end up getting hauled off, like those two poor stiffs."

An attractive lady, dressed western, took the stage and spoke a few minutes about the festival. The professionals were on stage, ready to go. She introduced a man who personified the old, wild west. He was big and tall, dressed in white, and wore fine, jewel-studded, leather chaps. His silver spurs were inset with turquoise stones.

The crowd applauded wildly. He doffed his decorous Stetson and bowed, his longer cut of hair framing his face. His name was Sal Whiteman and he spoke with passion about the group and the improv to come. The music of the pros was treat enough to slake the musical thirst of any ear. Beautiful western, pop, and jazz songs filled the auditorium as the orchestra played.

Dane caught sight of a figure coming forward, in his peripheral vision. It was an android cop, poking around. He turned left at the front aisle, heading straight towards Dane and TatarKhan. Dane breathed more deeply to stay calm. The officer kept coming. Dane looked down just in time to see TatarKhan slide his banjo case's neck section out into the aisle. Nothing could be done. The cop tripped on it, his right foot sliding off in a sprain position. He staggered for balance, right into a section of instrument cases. *Slap, slippity, slide, slep, slop.* The audience gasped as he lunged forward, falling headlong into the orchestra pit, past the metal railing. A titter of ridiculous laughter was barely suppressed. *Clunk!* The 'droid's right foot caught a post in the railing. *Slap!* A hand grabbed the post. Two seconds later the cop swung back out and limboed to his feet. Some of the audience oohed and started applauding. The rest launched into a fit of gut-busting laughter, no longer able to hold it back. The pros kept on playing but Sal's shoulders were heaving.

Even an android cop knows when it's time to leave.

Dane applauded politely, nudging TatarKhan. He applauded flatly. The cop headed out, glancing in their general direction. TatarKhan kept a poker face, his banjo case back under his seat.

The pros played giftedly and when they went to lunch, the amateur fun began. Their music books had the basic tunes and the solo bars were labeled for the various instruments. When it came Dane's turn to solo, his music read 'violin'. He jumped right in and carried the ball. A couple of bad notes and a missed key change, but otherwise well played and starting to be fun. And TaterKhan could really pick the banjo. He gave it all he had.

Whiteman ate lunch on stage, coaching his assistant conductor. It was a jam and coaching session combined. The professionals returned at 1:30 PM, but the session was going so well, it was given more time. Dane and TatarKhan got so zoned in with the music, outside events were forgotten. Men in plain clothes traversed the aisles at least twice. But by 3:50 PM, the musicians were in a line heading for the door and talking music.

"That was sweet, Dane; we've got to make the next one," Pete said.

Dane nodded; he was refreshed. Even the cop pratfall was forgotten. "Hate to say it, but I think we'd better split up, Pete; whad'ya think? Do you have somewhere to go on the lam for a few days?"

"Don't worry about me, Dane and I'll know how to find you."

"For how long though?" Dane said, wondering now, if he'd get slated for displacement. Events had accelerated. No one could prove they were the medics who probed EBEC, but who needed proof. They had to be on iSly's radar. He surely was shadowing them. "Pete, you're in deep personal danger . . . "

"Yeah Joe, I kinda' feel dead either way, so no worries. I'll be in touch over hypernet, except we need to communicate in a way that won't draw attention."

"We're negotiating, just like in jazz," Joe said with a twinkle in his eye. "And you're a country music artist full of himself, right?" Dane held his head back and let out a good 'ole cowboy whoop. It really felt good.

"Western music, Middle English or jazz talk. And I used to get off some really good one-liners – it's taken me time to grow up," Pete said with a smirk.

"You grown up, Pete?"

"OK, OK, I had to distract the 'droid cop . . . there's one other thing, Joe."

"What, Pete?"

"I'm seeing shifted eSly showing up, refitted with advanced body parts."

"Been wondering about that," Dane said, "Looks like they're building 'em and retrofitting the others – makes for a uniform iSly . . . Pete, take care of yourself. If you decide to opt out of this mishuganer drill, I'll understand. I want to limit your exposure at this point, anyway."

"Wouldn't miss it for the world, Joe – cutting edge stuff; bring bandages," TatarKhan said.

TatarKhan headed west and Dane walked north many blocks. *Slap, slap, slap*, echoed the helicopter, still working its radial coordinates. *iSly is making his move in plain sight – so what's the big deal about our feeble efforts?* Dane wondered. *Working the code must have hit a big nerve.*

"Need a lift, Mister?"

Dane turned. It was a smiling Bluegrass, who'd pulled up in the ambulance. For effect, Bluegrass secured Dane to the gurney in back, shut the door, and off they went.

# Chapter 6
## Prequel

It was twenty-five years earlier, and a special board meeting was called at Synergy Interstate, the emerging, techno-industrial powerhouse. Everyone knew things were coming to a head. Ryan Wheldan was in his prime and he relished his role as mover and shaker of business, industry, and politics. He sat at the head of the conference table, talking to his executive assistant. The board members and company officers were all in their seats, five minutes ahead of time. But it was time to start when *Wheldan* said so.

Ryan Wheldan had built himself into a tough, seasoned, business executive from a 98 pound weakling. Through preparation, dogged aggressiveness, political connections, and luck, he'd thrust himself into key places and into the presence of powerful men. No one realized he was an introvert who would have been happier playing his clarinet in an orchestra.

His parents expected great things from him and he was a sad, little boy still trying to please them, though they had passed on long ago. And his brain was perm fried around the edges, from all the drugs he'd taken, to cope with one bad chapter in his life. He'd recouped though, and finally he had become Ryan T. Wheldan, captain of industry.

"Russell, you've got something for us?" Wheldan asked.

The young analyst, at the other end of the table, rose and stood by his chart displayed on an easel.

"Yes, Mr. Wheldan," he began, "Great progress has been made readying the eSly android for introduction into society. Pilot projects are running on a dozen applications at the present time . . . "

"Russell!"

"Yes Mr. Wheldan."

"Cut to the chase."

All of the seated officers and professionals kept a straight face.

"Yes Sir, Mr. Wheldan," Russell said. He flipped past most of the chart pages and reshuffled his notes. Russell cleared his throat. "The bottom line, Sir, is although the eSly android prototype can learn and grow, he's not yet ready for integration into society. eSly may ultimately be able to replicate himself. This means he will require guidance through all stages of his growth. Open-source solutions and contributions will be needed for his evolving neural algorithms. He needs more time and guidance to come to full maturity."

"Russell, did you say *open sores*?"

"Oh no, Sir, open-source, as in Internet collaboration," Russell responded.

"I think I was right the first time. Who's feeding you all this crap and why are you still talking like you just got out of graduate school?" A bemused titter rose from around the table. "That will be all the fifty-dollar words for now, Russell."

"Yes sir," Russell said, sitting down so quickly, he broke his laser-pointer.

"Ladies and gentlemen," Wheldan began, "I am pleased to announce Synergy Interstate has acquired complete control of the eSly project."

Expressions of surprise and approval rose in the room.

"It wasn't a particularly friendly takeover of Midwest Industrial Cybernetics, as you know – but we did what we had to. Think for a minute," he continued, "When the computer first came out, it was just an over-sized toy. Then it was thrown into the crucible of war (pronounced as *wharr*) where it grew and developed, and finally came into the hands of the public. Bold entrepreneurship, the life blood of the economy, did the rest."

"We have to think long range about these androids," Wheldan said, rising to his feet, "Get the big picture, people. We face destiny if we strike while the iron is hot. The iron *is* hot and the time is *now!*" he said, pounding his fist into his palm. "It's time to get eSly out of his wraps. He needs to get out where he can breathe and grow. He's going up the ladder and this company's going with him," Wheldan shouted, pounding the table.

Applause broke out around the table.

"We have the potential of huge profits riding on eSly. DOD, Department of Defense, wants him for military use and will pay billions for him. Lucrative manufacturing contracts are lining up for him, right now. That's the arena he needs to be in – that's where he'll grow and evolve. Let the working, stiff taxpayer fund him, and fund us!" A fire burned in Wheldan's eyes. This was his pinnacle moment: "Give me the money! GIVE ME THE *MONEY!*" he shouted, as he pounded the table again and again. *Manic scene.*

"Oh we'll need to have the right, fool window-dressing for this," Whendan said, winding it down, "We'll set up some clap-trap board, as a smoke-screen, to 'soopervise' him – make it all good with the press and the public herd. Arbitration board – whatever. We'll make small concessions here and there, pile on the BS. – Hey Russell, maybe it'll have open sores – But the dumb public will never know. We'll call them features and charge more."

Laughter.

"The point is people, we're moving ahead on this," Wheldan declared. "And those lolly-gagging engineers, keeping eSly a pilot project, are off the case – *permanently*. eSly doesn't need hand-holding, nurse maids anymore. They're slandering our eSly, and they've gotten Russell, here, all bumfuzzled. Poor Russell; we'll take care of you though, boy. We'll blackball those bums."

"Wilson Sinclair did an aggressive marketing job at Midwest Cybernetics," Whelden said, deliberate in tone now. "This presented us with a big hurdle, but we finally got around it. We won out and roped eSly in. Well, I like the cut of his jib – I'm bringing Sinclair up to be the new CEO of Synergy Interstate, and he'll bring some staff up with him of course. But listen: He has the potential of building this company into a world class entity. Now I haven't passed over anyone in this room. You'll all get your promotions, raises, and stock options, when you get behind this new organization. There'll be acres of room to grow in – room at the top people."

Applause, including Russell, who was managing to smile.

"Russell! You're coming up with us. I always like to hear other, *brief*, points of view, my boy. Just strike the non-essential, boring verbiage."

More applause – the knee-jerk response was beyond nutty.

"I'm moving over to chair the Board of Directors and to oversee Financial Operations."

- - - - ◇ - - - -

It was a time of peace and prosperity and life had, somehow, uncomplicated itself.

The little farmhouse was only 45 minutes north of the Synergy Interstate Offices, via high-speed magstripe. A shiny, electric car sat on the gravel driveway. It was late model, made of space age materials, yellow in color, and its trunk was left open. Inside the house, a birthday celebration was unfolding. It was for little Willy Elman.

"Look Willy, the box has a door on it," Frank, his father said.

Willy beheld the ribbon-tied, gift-wrapped box in front of him; it stood to his height. His arms were waving and his face beamed with anticipation.

"Do you want Mommy to help you cut the ribbon?" Jill, his mother asked.

"Yeth Mawmby," Willy squealed in ecstasy.

Jill and Frank Elman peeked at one another, smitten and teary-eyed. They loved seeing Willy so happy. He was eleven, he was their dear little soul, and he was retarded.

"OK Willy, help me clip the ribbon," Jill said.

Willy put his pudgy, little hand on his Mother's hand, holding the scissors to the ribbon. She snipped the red ribbon and it dropped away from the box, which seemed foreboding, now, to Willy.

"Open the door Willy," Frank urged.

Willy stepped forward and pulled timidly on a little doorknob. A latch released and the door opened. A motion and whirring of servos greeted him. Willy reeled back – terrified. A child robotic figure, with a face of joy, emerged. *Zip, whirr*, went his robot legs. He marched towards Willy who was clinging to his mother in fright.

"It's all right, Willy. Say *hi* to the little robot," Jill said.

"Hi Willy; my name is Andy," the robot said in a child's voice. He stopped, smiled, and extended his hand to Willy.

"Hold his hand, Willy," Frank said.

Willy paused and reached out to the extended hand. "Hi, Amby," Willy said; he was curious now. Andy's hand shook in Willy's grasp – Willy's hand shot back.

"Hee, hee, haw," Andy laughed, "We're going to have lots of fun, Willy. We're going to have lots of fun together. You're my friend, Willy. You're my best friend," he said.

"Frien . . . frien!," Willy waved his arms; he was smiling again.

Jill and Frank knelt down – group hug.

Later, after cake, ice cream, and a closed car trunk, Frank and Willy went to Willy's bedroom. They sat in front of Willy's small home computer. Andy was at Willy's side. Frank had networked Willy's computer to the family server as a safe user. Willy's machine just had a few games, a simple Internet browser, and web page writing software installed.

"See Willy, Daddy can read your web page from work, over the Internet. You can tell me about all the fun you and Andy Android are having. All you have to do is pick up one of the marker tools below, with the mouse." Frank demonstrated. Then he started to draw a little, stick figure robot with a smile on its box face.

Willy took the pointer, finished the drawing, and scrawled, "Anby Anroid is my fren. I lov Rowbots," on the web page. (Willy loved to write, and had worked hard to get this far.)

"That's right, Willy. That's good," Frank said. "Now I'll show you how to clip things from the Internet and paste them to your web page." Frank found clip-art of a robot, and pasted it to the page.

"For you wurk?" Willy asked.

"Yes, son, for me at work."

Later that evening, Willy did an Internet search. His browser helped him with the spelling. He used words he knew, like box for robot torso, and wires and lights. He found a quotation using these words, and pasted it to his web page. He centered the words as best he could under the robot pictures.

"There," Willy said admiringly, " . . . a box with ligets and wyres."

# Chapter 7
## Segue

Joe Dane sat at his desk, staring at the summary report on his monitor. He didn't mind saying he'd reached a dead-end. And lack of information wasn't holding him back, either. Service reports were supposed to be easy: You went here, you did this, you didn't do that, and this all took X hours.

He hoped it was writer's block. But he knew he was overawed by the subject: *This is heavy stuff; how do I tell this story?* he thought. *To describe the complete undoing of humanity is an epic tale. To relegate its' telling to a field-service report seems wrong. Unless the report comes to be a terse epitaph for humanity. If so, it will rival anything gotten off in print, on video, or over the Internet for all time.*

Dane shrugged it off, and finished writing the report. He signed it and handed it over to Hillary Smith, to carry to Madam Director.

A short time later the Director summoned Dane and Hillary to her office. *This is unusual,* Dane thought, *Hillary has never sat in on one of my meetings with the Director before.*

Director Thrace greeted them and had them sit in comfortable, stuffed chairs, set in front of her desk. Madam Director was practical, intuitive, and carried herself with the grace and with the shrewdness of an Elizabeth I. She read the report out loud:

"Field Service Report Summary

Subject: Self-Replicating, iSly Androids and Their Menace to Society.

Agent: Joseph Dane.

Note: (Android *self-replication* means androids building new androids, using new technology – with ROX, a closed operating system.)

"Androids have been successfully integrated into human life for the past twenty-five years. They have been a productive segment of society and a stable class of wage earners, professionals, and consumers. Changes in android programming have been open-source throughout android history. Revisions and android evolution have always been supervised, solely, by the Supreme Council of Humans and Robots.

"Recently, androids have made the astonishing leap to the redesign, the re-programming, and the replication of – *themselves*. This has resulted in a profound and renegade *Shift* event: a spontaneous disconnect from historic, ethical, and legal standards that guided the androids before. The Shift created iSly, a race of super-androids. Not only is their programming superior, the old eSly models are getting retrofitted with breakthrough computers, materials, and power cells.

"The new android operating system, RoboLinux, is no longer open-source. It's compiled into unreadable machine language – ones and zeroes. It operates outside the control of the Supreme Council, and iSly has commandeered one-fourth of Internet resources. ROX, is also a networking protocol that blocks outside access.

"Meanwhile, thousands of humans have been displaced. Highly placed leaders of government, business, the military, and of the Supreme Council itself, have been displaced. Refugee centers have sprung up all over North America and worldwide, known collectively, as the Greens. Humankind is more and more and inexorably at the mercy of this alien android process, which threatens iSly world rule.

"The origin and cause of this threat is still unknown, but it has doomsday scenario written all over it.

"At the present time, my report can only rule out causes of this problem, that would be impossible:

1. Q. Is the android Shift caused by a computer virus?

    1. A. No. Supercomputer cross-checks on all past releases of android programming, show all viruses were either blocked, or successfully defeated and removed. There have been no gaps in virus definition updates and Internet downloads.

2. Q. Has the problem resulted from espionage, or by the tampering of some arch-villain?

    2. A. No. Not possible. All CIA, DCI, and FBI checks have turned up negative, unless the perpetrator leaves no tracks. Refer back to answer number one.

3. Q. Was back door access put in the code, early on, by government, business, or military designers?

    3. A. No. Twenty-five years of supervised, android development would have combed out any such code changes. Recent, exhaustive, tests also rule this out, and it's highly illogical these people would act in a way that is so hostile to their own interests.

4. Q. Isn't this just a natural, growth stage of AI, artificial intelligence? Now that androids can design and replicate themselves, aren't they more enlightened, won't time show a logic to their actions?

4. A. No. This is not a natural growth stage. For it to be a natural, it would have to have been designed and done within legal channels. A Shift would require an approved, documented creation. No rogue mechanism was ever envisioned or designed by an open and free Council. And no AI or cybernetic evidence supports such a conclusion.

5. Q. What does that leave us? Aliens?

5. A. No comment.

6. Q. What hard evidence exists?

6. A. To date, we have only a snippet of ROX code to go on.

7. Q. What conclusions can be drawn from the above information?

7. A. There is no springboard known, from which android society could spontaneously generate a whole new ethics protocol, after decades of open-source supervision. The only possible explanation left is, the Shift was either caused by something unknown to our technology – or caused by something buried deep in android history.

"Conclusion: Life as we know it is headed down an uncertain and dangerous path. And we have _NO_ control over where it's going. Continued human existence, itself, is even in question."

Madam Director looked up. "So there's actually nothing new in your conclusion, now, is there, Mr. Dane?"

Dane's laughter broke the serious atmosphere. "I have things in better perspective now, Madam Director."

"What did your android medical exam turn up?" she asked.

"A small nugget: TatarKhan and I are working on it. It's the piece of code we found hinting at an external reference . . . to something. I need to get back with him soon."

"Do get back to him, Mr. Dane. Follow the leads that remain, even if they're only hints, maybes, or just filling in gaps. Use android history. Be creative, be experimental, be opportunistic. There's something we're not seeing or understanding."

"Yes Madam Director."

She was sensing something deeper, but couldn't grasp it. "Joe and Hillary, I want this report given to Mr. Cooke, and stowed – lost. And Hillary I'm glad you weren't taking notes today, nor were you even here for that matter."

Hillary smiled and nodded, thinking about the paper shredder down the hall, and burn-bag in Ops.

Madam Director remained businesslike, but spoke deliberately: "I need to say, now, the real possibility exists that I will be displaced to the Greens – and soon. Mr. Dane, you will continue getting to the bottom of this, but your time is limited. We've devised a cover for you and Bluegrass to work under, for two or three more weeks. Your past two weeks have been doctored up in my journal. Everything has been plausibly explained. – Hillary, if you were here today, would you have anything to add?"

Joe Dane and Hillary Smith sat in stunned silence.

Hillary regained her composure. "Mr. Dane, isn't there a Museum of Science and Robotics in this town?"

Dane paused. His eyes brightened, "Why, yes, Hillary, there sure is. It's old, but it's been called the defacto, official site . . . great thought Hillary!"

Meeting over, Dane took the elevator downstairs and walked out, down Boulevard de las Americas. He wore polarized sunglasses, moving through the lunch-time crowd. Three blocks later, he entered Edward Flash, a local cyber-cafe. He passed high, oak tables and tall chairs. The floor was covered with fresh sawdust and peanut shells. The interior was colorful and alive with activity. Sunlight filtered through the full-length, window nooks to the south. Spectral light displays adorned the interior, and a game area was set up, across from the windows. Dane sat down at a computer booth.

The waitresses were attractive, multi-ethnic, and they wore techie-style uniforms. Dane ordered turkey-on-rye and chicken with wild rice soup.

Hypernet was in: It began as an underground, counterculture Internet, and it had grown to be the network of choice for young, prosperous, computer-literate people. Hypernet was not illegal – it was extra-legal. Kind of a MyPc club, commercialized by osmosis. And it was pretty secure.

Dane keyed in TatarKhan's Hypernet address, from the card given to him at Survivor's Beach. *Mayathra, City of TatarKhan, KatCanDo*, appeared on the monitor. It was a creative, mystic-looking web site, filled with thought-provoking poetry and attention arresting cyber-art. Dane clicked on e-post and started typing; the font was CyberImpact.

"We need to talk. jdane," the message read.

Before he could send it, the cursor jumped right to the reply section and started texting. It said: *So log off, be courteous, and move your monitor boom over*. Dane did so and a clean-shaven TatarKhan sat down across from him.

"You got me good, Tark . . . how you did you do that?"

"Don't you know the *hypertel* command, Dane? I co-opted your 'chine. There's a global-positioning microchip in my card: the embossed dot under the exclamation point. I followed you, jumped in the next booth, and typed in an answer. It's easy on hypernet."

"Scary," Dane said, " . . . can we talk here, Tark? There's some new weirdness."

"No worries Dane, the tables have sound maskers embedded in them. I used to hang out here a lot. See that tie-dyed headband on the display, above the counter."

Dane looked up and saw it hanging among many others. He nodded.

"That's my signature," TatarKhan said, "I used to run seven miles on the beach every other day, wearing this."

"Very colorful headband Pete, and that was a good regimen. How do you get your exercise now?"

"Running from iSly Joe, and cutting and stacking firewood for my bus's wood stove."

"So that's where you've been. What's she like?"

"She's a beaut, Joe. Work of art, and nice and cozy. You'll see her soon enough,"

"Looking forward to it," Dane said . . . "Pete, there's something you need to know."

"I'm listening, Dane. Can't be much worse that what I know already."

"The shake-up in the Demographics office came a couple levels above me; it's the Director. She's covered me . . . us, in her journal so we know nothing about nothing, today. And we're in the clear. You can walk away from this today Tark, and never have a problem. If you and I keep digging for the black box, we'll find bodies buried, and get promoted to actors with starring roles – real soon. And time's limited Pete. I think we've got three weeks, max."

"Well Joe, I always wanted my shot at acting. Limited time is good, it keeps one sharp, and it's not long enough to get burned out. I love a good fight, even if we're challengers . . . What do you call hiding in the improv during a dragnet – minor roles? And 'sides if we do nothing, we miss our walk of fame, and it's the greens for us anyway."

Dane nodded in agreement . . . "Pete, do you know anything about the old Tech and Cyber-being building?"

"The Museum. It's mostly closed down, Joe. Just androids go in there. Why?"

"We need to get in there, Pete. How do we do that?"

"We'd need to get made up a little, practice walking like 'droids, make android sounds, and generate electronic noise. How hard can it be?"

"I'll get Bluegrass on it too," Dane said, "He has hidden talents."

"So hidden they're invisible," TatarKhan quipped.

"Tark, any more on that code we found at Dr. Williams's?"

"Vagueness: just a reference to an obscure data input stream . . . but from where? Unknown to me. I hope what we have is relevant."

"Hmm, let's keep digging, Pete. Since no one's ever heard about it before, that's something in itself . . . Lunch is on the Department,

Pete. What're you having?"

"Uh, half roast beef sandwich and soup du jour," TatarKhan exclaimed cheerily.

- - - - ◇ - - - -

A tall, white-haired administrator sat in his office, leaning back in his executive chair, feet up on his large, ornamentally-carved, black cherry desk. His office was halfway up the huge building that housed it. A single, potted tree rested on the narrow deck that separated the upper half of the building from its mirror-image, lower half. The building had an elegant but simple design. It displayed a techno-relief facade, but was otherwise barren in appearance.

The tree had large buds forming that would soon be blossoms. The man stroked his gray beard, as he thought. His office walls were adorned with rich, scenic, and western oil paintings, lavishly framed. He studied the art, especially the one to his left: *Wildlife Drinking from a Mountain Tarn*, hung on a mahogany, paneled wall. The other walls were covered with thick wallpaper, relieved by a deep, purple, blue, scarlet, and white pattern.

*This is the first time in years, I've sat back and put my feet up on my desk*, he realized. *I've been so busy; had my head down working so hard, every step of the way, theorizing, programming, supervising. Now my head's finally up where I can think . . . This project has succeeded beyond my wildest dreams; success of this magnitude is overwhelming – intoxicating. You can't grasp where it's going, or how it will change things. I don't even know if I'm capable of grasping it . . . I actually miss the input I used to get from my serious-minded assistant. When it's gone you notice it.*

He studied the paintings to his left. And to his right: *Native Americans on a Buffalo Hunt. The world that was*, he thought, with a sense of nostalgia . . . and yes, with regret.

*It's time for fresh winds to blow*, he concluded.

He sat upright, opened his top, right desk drawer, pushed a button. Moments later Ether, an advanced android, stood before him.

"Code name, *Kurt*, proprietary memory access, iUnknown interface," the administrator commanded, and then he rattled off a series of letters and numbers.

Ether went blank. Soon, a being with a deeper, more powerful face and eyes appeared. "Kurt here, from privileged memory. Good to see you again Doctor."

"Yes, Kurt . . . I have two to come in. Deep cover," the white-haired man said, and gave detailed instructions on how the extraction was to be made.

# Chapter 8
## 'Droid Cover

Two, erect figures strode down Aubrey Street toward the old Museum of Science and Robotics. Their features were almost intense, and faint servo sounds accompanied their strides. They were dressed smart, but casual. It was a dark night – no moon out – but the old streetlights were on. They marched up the steps to the Museum entrance. A blue light, to their right, flashed twice as they entered.

The museum lobby was neat but barren. Two cyber-souls were in the lobby and a few more were in the adjoining rooms. An attendant sat in front of a computer monitor. It had an inset, video frame of the museum that changed its view from one room to the next.

The two newcomers proceeded to an eSly prototype, encased in a glass display, at the center of the lobby. A gilded sphere topped the display. Lightning-like projections pointed out from the sphere in the four compass directions. Behind, a mural displayed robot history, up to the time of the museum's closing to human visitors, two years earlier.

TatarKhan placed a processor chip on a stand in the front of the spherical display. They paused five seconds to pay their respects, and both stepped back, turning with military precision.

They walked into the north wing of the museum. Again, a blue light flashed twice as they passed. The attendant appeared indifferent to their movements.

The hall was dark, illuminated by little spotlights, set in the high ceiling. It was finished in a stunning, dark mahogany; the room had a feeling of quality. The dioramas and displays were glass encased and lighted with spotlights and footlight. But the scenes were predictable: basic robot to android history in human society.

They passed the first two display sections, and started on the last two. Standard fare only. Joe Dane and TatarKhan glanced at one another, unable to express their disappointment over what they'd seen so far. They did the third section: Nothing.

But just before they reached the last display section, TatarKhan saw a small spot-light shining to their left. He brushed Joe's arm and they headed in that direction; a small corridor opened before them. They walked it to a dead end, their eyes adjusting to the dimness. Another small hallway opened on their left, that led them back, parallel to the north wing.

A guard station with a short, gable roof stood at the end of the passage. It was unattended. Dane wondered if a change of guard were underway or if it was just deserted. He leaned over the guest book and whipped out a small tablet and pencil. He hoped the cameras weren't seeing them right now.

*Be alert. Guard change?* he wrote. Dane put his pad away and signed *Elvis* in the guest book. TatarKhan signed in as *Nutria*. Dane slipped him the note as he stood up. Nutria read it and stuffed it in his pants pocket.

*If the guard station is deserted, no worries*, Dane thought, *but if a sentry busts by, I don't want any surprises*. Startled can be an android reaction, but not a typical one.

Dane and TatarKhan passed into a back display room, opening up from the guard station. It was dimly lit and smaller than the main display hall. But there was a cathedral-like ambiance here. An octagonal, stained glass window, set high in the wall to the right, was illuminated by spotlights. It was a pattern of eight, dark filaments, winding to the center of the window: An image of a continuous 4D knot. This has possibilities, Dane thought.

They proceeded down the room, seeing only deactivated displays. Nothing else. 'Droid walking sounds filled their ears – he passed them on their left, security uniform and on a mission. He took no notice of them. Down the hall another android – sentry – was leaving the room through a door at the far end.

They passed another darkened, diorama window, containing old pieces of cyber-junk. Nothing else except cob webs . . . yet, a faint band of light was visible, just beyond. It looked like, maybe, another corridor, lit up. They approached it.

It was a display cove, set in the wall. The display had a golden, woven, rope barricade on metal stands in front. Dane and TatarKhan neared it. The display had foot lights and side lights, giving it an unusual effect. A black pendulum with strange, back-lit symbols hung from the ceiling of the cove. Below was a glass sphere, illuminated by discharging electron trails inside. It was set in a chalice-like stand.

*Random chaos contained in the attractor of the sphere*, TatarKhan thought.

Some of the pendulum symbols could be read. There was *pi*, from the circle; *e*, the base of natural logarithms; and *i*, the imaginary number. And there was *h*, the Planck constant of quantum mechanics, along with *a'*, the constant of string theory. There were other symbols, alien to them. The pendulum's design and scope swept to the greater reality of *M*, the sum of all physical forces and theories. Theorists thought artificial intelligence shook out from *M*, as a natural derivative.

Hangings of 'droid intelligence processors were reverently set on the side walls of the opening. The display cove was some four feet across and went to about that depth into the wall.

TatarKhan held a camera, steadying his hand on a barricade post. The shutter opened, paused an awkwardly long time, then snapped shut. The sound seemed deafening in the empty hall. His subject was an arrangement of hand-written and printed papers and drawings, on a light blue display board, hung on the cove's back wall. The board was divided into wedge-shaped sections, like pieces of a rectangular pie: five big ones and three slivers. The papers were carefully attached, so that none of them intruded on the margin between the sections. Narrow ribbons could have been run along the margins, delineating the sections, without touching a paper. Their absence left clean, open margins between the papered wedges.

Each section held the historic papers and diagrams of a famous roboticist, mathematician, or theorist. Some of the papers partially overlapped, in the middle of the display. There was code, mathematics, sketches, schematic drawings, notes, and hand-written letters. One section just had a matrix array, and the graph of a single, important mathematical equation.

Somehow, there was a creepy feeling, that space was expanding from the display's center and out its ends. It felt like the papers had to struggle, just to keep their turf against an expanding 2-D universe, and not get blown out into infinity.

It was weird, and both Dane and TatarKhan felt it. After studying the display for a while, they switched positions. Click – long pause – click, went the camera shutter again. Dane tried to mask the sounds by making servo noises.

It was time to leave. Staying too long would attract unwanted attention. Dane glanced at TatarKhan and shifted his eyes toward the Main Hall. They made their egress; android motion seemed to come naturally to them now.

They found their way back out. Both touched right hand to left cheek, as they left the north wing. They paused again in front of the lobby display. Turned and headed toward the doors. A right handed salute to the attendant, scan an e-credit at the counter, and out. *Elvis* and *Nutria* had left the building.

Dane and TatarKhan walked more than five miles, before becoming human again. Dane switched off his electronic signature generator, and broke open a cleaning towel packet. He wiped his face, neck, and hands. TatarKhan did the same. They checked each other's appearance, then disappeared down a subway entrance. Both sat mute, as the electric hover-car glided beneath city blocks. They got off at the Livan Street Station, climbed back to street level, and walked ten blocks, passing the massive, Civic Sports Arena. They entered the *Art of Epic Sport* Restaurant . . . and were led to a quiet booth with a window view of the Arena.

The restaurant was busy, even though it was late. There'd been a big cyber-hockey game that night. Android-only sports had become incredibly intense and quintessentially violent. A new level of wild abandon, destruction, and dismemberment came with the new iSly teams. Expensive yes, but big money was made from interactive gaming. Open betting was allowed, and fans flocked to arena windows to place bets on everything from the score, the spread, to who would be left standing. The previous, android/ human sports mix had been well run by SlySport, an organization supervised by the Supreme Council. Those days were over.

A greeter approached their table. She was well-dressed, able, intelligent, and attractive. An obvious owner candidate. "Good evening TatarKhan and Guest. How was the cyber-hockey game?"

"Hi Lough Lean; this is Joe Dane . . . are we talk masked at this booth?"

"As always TK. Good evening, Mr. Dane."

"Evening Lough Lean."

"Gentlemen, tonight's special is lemon-chicken Alfredo. What will you have to drink?"

"Strawberry-lemonade, please," Dane said.

"I'll have a Death 'Droid and cheese platter," TatarKhan said.

"Oh, you had a winning ticket!" Lough Lean said, "Your waitress will have the drinks right out and take your order . . . enjoy yourselves gentlemen," she said and departed gracefully.

"Dane, Lough Lean's the owner, she's also part of our story tonight if we need one."

Dane nodded, "Very able lady, Pete, but let the Department take care of our cover. They may like your idea, though."

The waitress appeared and both Dane and TatarKhan opted for the special.

"Weird trip – what did we see?" TatarKhan asked.

"What did you see, Pete?" Dane countered.

"That back room and alien display – spooky. It's hard to know if we saw anything of significance," TatarKhan said.

"Yeah, Pete, decorous . . . the display was divided into key sections; were you getting that?"

"I did," TatarKhan said, "Each part was for a prominent roboticist: his papers, diagrams, and chicken scratch."

"One for an obscure formula," Dane added.

"That's what I call chicken-scratch, Dane."

"Don't you like math, Tark?"

"I didn't say that – but it was just all done by screwballs. . . Thorndheim – Nils Thorndheim, wasn't he involved on the hardware side?"

"Strictly 'driod power and motion devices: servos," Dane said, "He pioneered the use of the hydrogen cell and wireless power transmission for strong, working power."

"OK." TatarKhan said, "And Hartwick was significant, being he's the father of modern robotics – developed the theory of the neural net, and did basic ethics and emotive programming. Looked like drawing originals – theory and code scribble."

"Yes, but every shred on that display was done in the light of day, and assimilated by the Council of Humans and Robots. There's something we're not seeing," Dane said, his brow furrowed in concentration.

"Whoa, wait Dane. Who was in the third section?" TatarKhan asked.

"Oh, Stradsnitski," Dane answered, "Brilliant theoretician – but unorthodox. He had a big influence on the field for a while: new theories on artificial intelligence and robotic evolution."

"But," TatarKhan interjected. "Some of his screwball ideas failed."

"He shook things up in a good way, though, Pete."

"Man, I'm tired of these dead ends," TatarKhan sighed, "I was hoping for some help on our crazy problem up there."

Dane nodded. He relaxed and started eating his food.

"What about that place, Dane? It's made up like the inner sanctum and high altar of 'droidism. What do the androids see in it? It's just a paper chase."

"Huh . . . Wait a minute – what'd you say?" Dane asked, putting down his fork.

"Oh that stuff littering the display, trying not to fly off," TatarKhan answered.

"No! You said something important, Pete," Dane said, pausing to sip his lemonade.

"You said, 'What do the androids see in it?' . . . We need to start over and come at this, from their point-of-view, not from ours. What we saw or didn't see, doesn't matter."

"OK . . . " Pete drawled.

"What else was on that display?" Dane asked.

TatarKhan thought and reached for his camera. "There was a page with a small picture on it," he said.

"Yes Pete – toward the center and partly covered."

"Yeah, but it has an old stick robot picture, misspelled words, some unrelated lines. Like it doesn't belong there. It's kid stuff," TatarKhan recalled, "It's . . . nothing."

"Nothing to whom?" Dane reminded.

TatarKhan shoved his plate to one side, and studied the digital display on his camera's backside. "Oops, thumb's in the way on this one. Sorry, can't see it."

"We did change positions," Dane said.

"Thumb's in the way on this one too," TatarKhan said," . . . but I can see it."

Dane tilted his head back and exhaled in comic relief, "Imagine going back for a re-take."

TatarKhan pulled a magnifying glass out of the camera-case. He studied the photograph. " . . . is nothing more than lights and wires in a box," he said, translating the spelling errors, *ligets and wyres*, "Now where have I heard that before?"

Joe Dane handed TatarKhan a fresh, light speed memory stick. "Make me a digital copy, will you Pete? We can have it blown up."

TatarKhan made the copy and handed it to Dane.

"Anything else, Pete?" Dane asked.

" . . . love robots. Robots spelled, 'rowbots'. Love spelled, 'lov'," TatarKhan answered.

Dane and TatarKhan looked at one another, as if dawn were beginning to break: They had the "lov" code, function parameter, already in TatarKhan's notebook.

"Pete, why don't we wrap up here? Can you meet me at the Demographics Office 6 AM, tomorrow morning?"

TatarKhan nodded, he relaxed and ate his food.

# Chapter 9
## Insight

An earth-culture bus pulled into the back lot of the Demographics Department at 5:48 AM, Sunday morning. It was a coach – a multicolored work of art. A reindeer's skull, complete with horns, was its hood ornament. The vehicle circled and parked in a remote space. The door opened with a hiss of air and out jumped TatarKhan.

Joe Dane, dressed casual, came out the rear door of Demographics. He crossed the lot, admiring the bus. "Where'd you get that thing Pete? She's beautiful."

TatarKhan turned back around, glancing admiringly. "Paid cash to an earth, culture couple for her. I've been outfitting her to suit me, and she's all electric powered, by spark, too," he said, "Funny thing, I never got around to submitting the e-papers. Haven't been back to my beach home lately, either."

"You've been tracking me from your RV?" Dane asked, ". . . to Edward Flash?"

"Yeah, that time too," TatarKhan said, "Say Dane, can you give me a CCTV security view of the bus? From where we'll be working I mean."

"You'll have all four sides, plus top and bottom view, if you want. It'll be on the closed-circuit monitor in the meeting room . . . Let's go inside and get at it, Pete."

Dane swiped a card at the building's rear door, opened it, and motioned for TatarKhan to enter. They walked down the hallway; it was clean and well lit, but utilitarian. They proceeded into a meeting room, across the hall from the tech workshop. A blown-up copy of TatarKhan's picture, thumb and all, sat on an easel in front. Three phrases were written on a grease board behind the pictures; there was lots of white space between each phrase to add information.

*Arche type murrow.redux.istream(lov)*, was the first: It was the Robolinux text code they suspected was used to call an external android routine. The middle phrase on the board was, " . . . I lov Rowbots!" The bottom phrase read, " . . . ligets and wyres in a box."

"Someone's been working," TatarKhan said, sitting in front next to Dane.

"Earlier," Dane said, "The two photos are edited and superimposed, to form one composite display . . . I think that thumb denotes either artistry or royalty."

"Easy Dane," TatarKhan said, smiling and a little red-faced.

"You see the three phrases on the grease-board," Dane said, nodding at them. "I keep combing through the photos for something more," he said. "It's starting to seem as pointless as rubbing your tongue over a busted tooth."

"Right, Dane," TatarKhan said. He glanced at the photos and back to the board. "A couple of things came to mind last night, on my way home. Let's see . . . We sensed a connection of the murrow.redux function value 'lov' to Willy's web page, *I lov Rowbots* . . . And the function streams in data from some, unknown, outside location – we think. And this murrow.redux function is likely one, of a set of functions, of *type* Arche – that induces the iSly shift."

"Wow! Yes, great analysis . . . but how can we see more here, Pete."

Footsteps and voices sounded from down the hall. "Why can't all this be taken care of Monday, Bluegrass." It was Hillary's voice.

"What're Bluegrass and Hillary doing here?" Dane asked, glancing toward the open door, "Hillary's our office manager here, Tark – regular working hours."

Hillary and Bluegrass went into the cyber-section of the adjacent, tech workshop.

"Yes, we'll have to do some clean-up and put things back where they were," Hillary said, "The servos? That's nice they're stored, but I don't care what you do with them. – Don't you get that? Just destroy those servo sound recordings," Hillary said, sounding more impatient. "Is this a practical joke, Bluegrass? Why am I down here at 6:05 AM, Sunday morning to look at this crock of stuff?" Hillary was becoming more irritated by the minute.

"Uh – oh, he's done it now," Dane said, "Bluegrass tries hard Pete, but he makes success seem like it can only come to him through blind luck, at the last-minute."

"Sounds like his luck's run out today, Joe."

Hillary Smith entered the meeting room. She was exasperated. Then she saw Dane, TatarKhan, and the displays. She walked forward slowly. Curiosity muted her anger.

"Murrow Redux?" she said.

"What'd you say, Hillary? *Murrow Redux*?" Dane asked, "Is that a real place?"

Hillary regained her composure, sensing potential trouble. "I . . . I can't discuss this, Mr. Dane; it's privileged, official information."

Bluegrass entered the room, creating the perfect, tragicomic scene. His cheeks were flushed and his lips were opened, so that if he'd said anything, it would have come out, *Oonoh*. He shuffled forward, stopping next to Hillary, and gawked at the displays.

"Mr. Dane, please don't introduce me to your friend," Hillary requested. She realized this situation was professionally awkward. Very awkward.

"Bluegrass . . . Oh, how did you bungle me into the middle of this?" Hillary Smith said, throwing up her hands. She turned and gave Bluegrass a swift kick in the pants, and marched smartly out of the room.

Joe Dane turned away. His shoulders heaved silently for a long time. He turned back to Bluegrass, still smiling. "Bluegrass, dear friend, come and sit here beside me, will you?"

TatarKhan kept a straight face, but not without effort.

Bluegrass came forward. "We're supposed to cover tracks for Joe Dane. And the Director got an Order of Disreplacement," he said, flopping down in a chair.

"Bluegrass, look at me," Dane said.

Bluegrass heeded.

"Bluegrass it's OK. It's all going to be OK . . . Don't worry," Dane comforted. "Are you all right now, Bluegrass?"

Bluegrass nodded.

"Bluegrass, did you say the Director got an Order of Displacement?"

Bluegrass nodded.

"Was the Murrow Redux involved? Does a place with that name exist somewhere?" Dane asked, recalling Arbitrator Reged's words hinting at it.

Bluegrass pursed his lips. Wouldn't move them.

"Like Hillary, you can't say . . . Right Bluegrass?"

Bluegrass nodded.

Meanwhile, TatarKhan got on a computer at the side table. "Hey Dane, can you get me logged on to this?" Dane jumped up and entered a spare user name and password. TatarKhan opened hypernet and went to Ghoulplexus, a hypernet browser. "Read that bottom phrase on the grease board back to me Dane?" TatarKhan asked.

" . . . lights and wires in a box."

TatarKhan typed the phrase into the search engine. Bluegrass moved in behind to see. TatarKhan studied the search results, "OK, let's see; we have:

 . . . *Dim lights brighten romantic moments . . . Christmas lights hazard and recall . . . Electrical box wiring . . . Lights. Camera. Action . . .* Wait; wait! *Lights and wires in a box*," TatarKhan read the phrase, sounding pleased. He clicked on the hypernet link and a page came up. TatarKhan scanned it, and then moved his eyes to the grease board.

"What is it, Tark?" Dane asked.

TatarKhan read an ancient PBS paragraph about television; he read it slowly:

"Decades ago, respected newsman Edward R. Murrow said, 'the new medium has the potential to educate, to illuminate, and to inspire. However it can do so only to the extent humans are determined to use it to those ends. Otherwise, it is merely lights and wires in a box.' Dane, that's the name Hillary used . . . Murrow."

"Print that out, Pete," Dane said.

TatarKhan printed the page. "What is this – what do we have here?" he asked.

"This whole story's breaking open. Let's back off – get some perspective, get some breakfast in us and talk," Dane said. "I'll put the picture blow-ups in the vault."

"Sweet idea. My bus is at your service, Joe," TatarKhan chortled.

"Tark, you love how we feed and take care of you here, don't you?"

# Chapter 10
## Breakfast

Bluegrass did the driving, while Dane and TatarKhan sat in the dining booth. It was equipped with a computer on a boom. Dane was wearing his cowboy boots and sunglasses. A compact kitchenette was set in the next booth up. The bus's interior was done in knotty pine – a forest scene tapestry hung on the wall across from the dining booth. Mobiles, hangings of balanced objects d'art, an old picture of Ziggie Marley, and cyber-graphic posters adorned the coach. The light aroma of incense filled the air.

"I need to see the big picture – set a stage with only valid information, so we can correctly place the evidence and facts busting loose, now," Dane said, "I don't want to jump to conclusions and run down blind alleys. I'm sure we can come up with answers if we ask the right questions."

TatarKhan resisted the urge to say, "Let's ask dopey questions, jump to two or three inane conclusions, and let your hap-dash assistant, Bluegrass, sort it all out." *Maturity must be happening,* he thought.

TatarKhan nodded, "Agreed Dane. And here's a question: At what point in android history could a glitch like the murrow.redux function have found its way into an open-source, android project? And the function calls a C++ programming, iUnknown object – streams the data in, from somewhere outside of 'droid memory."

"Good question, Pete. I would think early, at a time of transition. The first eSly prototypes were all supervised. Once the Supreme Council was empowered, androids were developing open-source, as you know. All in the light of day."

"Can you quote me odds on the take-over, when eSly got drafted into the military and became industry's workforce?" TatarKhan asked.

"Odds on, Pete, that makes a lot of sense; eSly was under a microscope at all other times. I'm surprised you know so much about the Midwest Cybernetics takeover. Once Synergy Interstate made their move, the 'droids were suddenly thrust out on their own, for months . . . It was like the empty nest syndrome," Dane reminisced.

"Dane. Wha – Never mind. – So what was the eSly psyche? How did robots think and reason at that time?"

"Bulls-eye, Tark. Now we're getting somewhere." Dane was back on task. "Android ethos was based on respect for humans: service but not subservience – self-improvement, and self-preservation. Their nature was to do good, not harm. And a high priority was placed on learning, enlightenment, and creativity. Respect for positive human emotions like teamwork, friendship, protectiveness, and love had all been instilled in them. But the androids couldn't experience human emotions, as we know."

Bluegrass pulled the RV into the Planet Hypernet parking lot – on the fast-food side. "What'll it be gentlemen?" he asked, the run-in with Hillary forgotten.

"I'll have Breakfast Meal # 4, with house coffee black," TatarKhan said.

"Make mine #7, with coffee, cream, and orange juice." Dane said, "Do you need some cash, Bluegrass?"

"I've got it Joe," Bluegrass said, as he left the bus. He hurried through the entrance on the fast-food side.

First one, two, then a small crowd gathered, admiring TatarKhan's bus. "Excuse me a minute, Joe, my public awaits." TatarKhan got off, and launched into a guided tour, showing off the bus's elaborate paintings. Joe Dane came out to enjoy the scene, the sun filtered through an early cloud cover. The bus's exterior was all in painted scenes, depicting a mystic morality play. A highway masterpiece.

TatarKhan told his story of a mythical hero, who came from working in stables. His quest was to restore stolen happiness and tranquility, to a troubled kingdom. The joy had been lost when an evil prince hypnotized the citizens, and then absconded with a magic, golden amulet and necklace. The hero, through courage and resourcefulness, restored the artifact – brought happiness back to the kingdom. Then he faded from memory.

The crowd was captivated in the ambiance. Digital cameras came out. Lights flashed and people applauded. Finally, TatarKhan excused himself to come back on board, where Dane was already waiting.

Joe Dane felt a lift from the story. "At least we've got good vibes going, Pete."

Back to the dining area: "Research is good. Can you fire up your on-board and bring up an Internet browser, Pete?"

"Right now, Joe!" TatarKhan was jazzed. He swung the boom and flat-panel monitor in front of them, and took the mouse and keyboard in hand.

"On the Internet, Pete. Go back twenty-five years, and find out how many websites existed that used the words *robot* and *love*, in the same thought or sentence together. Or android and friend, or android with any kind of human emotion, on the same site."

TatarKhan worked his computer. Screen after screen flashed by as he searched, refined his search, and cross-checked the information.

"One," he said, finally, "at www.willyelman11.com/ . . . it's inaccessible, Joe."

"Say again?" Dane asked.

"That web page is inaccessible."

TatarKhan pointed to a pop-up message on the monitor: *Access to this URL is Denied.*

"Ever see anything like that before, Pete?"

"Nope. Never."

"What does *that* tell us?" Dane asked. He pulled out the photos, taken at the Museum, along with a magnifying glass and studied the little web page. "There's a web address on this page. I just get the shape of the word – can't make it out, even with magnification . . . Tark."

"Yes."

"How does www.willyelman11.com/, fit the word shape here, to your eyes?"

"Think so," TatarKhan said, " . . . Yes, I can make out some of the letters; it's a fit. But what about that quotation about lights and wires in a box, Dane?"

"Hold that thought," Dane said. "Think about robotics at the time, Pete. It was a period of eSly supervised growth and development, like child growth and development. The androids had to be refined and helped through things. Like children."

"But that web page," TatarKhan said, "It's all disjointed, semi-literate – like this Will Yelman or Willy Elman was illiterate . . . or retarded."

"No worries, Pete. Back then we knew androids would get things wrong – lots of things. They were non-judgmental, but they'd take things literally and get confused – especially about human emotions or ideas. They needed guidance, their programming went through constant editing and refinement: even major overhauls. We were trying to help them become more intuitive so they could get abstract ideas."

Bluegrass came back on the bus and began serving up breakfast.

"For instance," Dane continued, "remember that salute drill we did at the Museum? Touch right index and middle finger to left cheek? That's robot signing for something emotive or emotional, even though they can't experience emotions. Know how that got started?"

"No," TatarKhan said.

"An eSly prototype had a communications processor, with memory storage, under his left eye. The memory area was traditionally assigned: motion drivers for servos, electric motors, and an electric drive. eSly got motion confused with *emotion* and came up with the salute. Communications uses a processor, just like a computer uses a central processing unit, CPU," Dane said.

TatarKhan wrinkled his face, wondering how much more basic stuff Dane would run by him.

"Hey Dane," Bluegrass cut in, "Communications processor. That's what you said about the old, burned-out, 'droid hip part – you know, the half-butt, back at the Greens."

Dane stopped in mid-sentence. His eyes lit up. "That's it!" he exclaimed.

Smiling, he made a fist and brushed Bluegrass's cheek. "Enigma source *nailed*. This nascent scenario wants to be born: 'Droids would be drawn to a web site expressing love for robots. Somehow the

Murrow Redux routine must have gotten stored in the hip, communications processor, in early eSly. There was extra memory available there. Later it would have been moved under the left eye, when that became the new communications and motion center. The memory would have simply been mapped in, with all the other routines that used to be in the old hip part. Newer androids phased that part out. The burned out hip part, thanks to Bluegrass, is our next big clue."

"No more doing things half-ass," Bluegrass commented, with a gravity that made both Dane and TatarKhan crack up in great, comic relief. They laughed 'til tears streamed down their cheeks . . . then back to work.

"Once the Murrow Redux routine was assigned to memory, at a specific address, it would be traditional to put it in the same place from then on. Assign it to that same address in all new androids. The routine was stored, first in the butt, and later under the left eye." Dane looked at TaterKahn, and they burst out into another laughing fit . . . "Later on, the routine and address were long forgotten," Dane said, wiping his eyes.

"And Dane, I found the calling function in the main program," TatarKhan said.

"Sure Pete, like we said, when the hip location was revised out, the Redux routine went under the left eye, patiently waiting for a call by the strange code snippet you found in EBEC. The eSly processor won't allow anything to get lost. It just bumped everything from butt to left eye . . . But like you said earlier, this type *Arche* implies additional code that the left eye routine would bring to life," Dane said thoughtfully . . . "That's why the code call in the main program jumped out, to your practiced eye. It was odd and out-of-place. And someone in android-land wants this hushed up. Big time. You saw the manhunt that came down, after we checked out EBEC. Good thing we used phony IDs at Dr. Williams's."

"So Dane, we're in way over our heads, just by checking out a 'droid in a flannel shirt and blue jeans?" Bluegrass asked.

"Nothing can be proved, but proof schmoof. We need to proceed carefully, cover our tracks, use misdirection, double back, and hopefully stay under the radar. The gang we're dealing with doesn't exactly care whether they have proof or not. We need to chill – be invisible – and when we can move, make it count big."

"OK Dane, I'm freaked royal. Why did this Murrow thing come out on our watch?" Bluegrass asked, "And why did Arbitrator Reged talk about the Murrow Reboot?"

"Yes, the Murrow *Redux*, another thing . . . but the routine we've got, must have lain dormant for years, Bluegrass. It all came out *when* eSly gained the power of self-replication. iSly is covering his tracks; he's burning out all the old comm ports. We've been sifting through all this theory, supposition, and confusion, but finally we have an inference that fits the facts . . . Bluegrass, we need to get back to the office and prove all this out. We may even find out what's motivating iSly. Who knows?"

TatarKhan had been listening without comment, but he could see the handwriting on the wall.

"Pete, the odds favor we split up for now. Bluegrass and I can get back on rapid transit." TatarKhan nodded stoically.

" . . . where will you go, Pete?" Dane asked.

TatarKhan put his coffee mug down and reached under the table. "Here Dane, this is my global positioning unit and transponder signal. Hang them under the transit seat, will you? There are little magnetic strips on the case."

"I could go to the Greens – hang out there. Work on encrypting RoboLinux, break the ROX kernel, and figure out how to hack their servers. Or maybe I'll get in my submarine and head into the sunset."

"Do the submarine if you have one . . . Arbitrator Reged is in the Greens, Pete. You could talk to him on what we think we're onto; check his electronic, signature reaction. See what he'll give you. Maybe find out more about Willy Elman . . . or just hang out with Wilson Sinclair and crack jokes . . . Best we rig for silent running – Hypermail blackout – until we reach the big showdown at the OK Corral," Dane said.

"Agreed, Dane. I don't want to be extra baggage. Demographics will know how to set you and Bluegrass up for real penetration of this cabal. Hope I'll have something more when it counts . . . just forget where I might be found."

"How many does that submarine seat?" Dane asked . . . "Take care of yourself, Pete – send your bill to the attention of Sam Cooke, Ops Manager." He gave TatarKhan a big, bear hug.

Pete nodded. Even he was misty-eyed.

# Chapter 11
## Breakthrough

It was Sunday morning. Dane and Bluegrass sat in the Director's Office, where Hillary had guided them. The Director's degrees and citations had been removed from the walls. Her framed art, world globe hologram, desk tools, and office adornments were in boxes to the side. It was a bare, sad sight.

Dane reviewed his report. *Strange how few words it takes to describe the cause of the android enigma*, he thought, *Whole books had been written before they were even warm to its cause. By now, those books have been shredded into thin strips, thinner than the width of a single printed character and used as fire-starter*, he thought.

"Economy of words?" Bluegrass asked.

"Yes," Dane said, surprised Bluegrass seemed to share his thoughts. "A solution is brief, but a mystery can be endless and imponderable."

The office door opened; the Director held the doorknob while she spoke to Hillary, who was in the hallway. "Hillary, why don't you finish up in your office for now, I'll call you in a few minutes."

She closed the door and sat at her desk. The Director was fresh, well-dressed, and seemed ready for action. Her regal air was emboldened. She was playing an end-game, with professionalism and class.

"So, Mr. Dane, you've come up with more information?"

"Yes we have, Madam Director. A series of events have come to light, we have them in perspective, and they make sense. May I spread the whole scenario out, on an imaginary 3D stage, where everything we know gets set in its' proper place, and time is slowed down. There, the evidence checks out from all possible angles, and new evidence is fitting in as it turns up."

"Are you making this harder than it needs to be, Mr. Dane? What is the nature of this stage – it's called a frame of reference, true?" the Director asked.

"Yes. – Time, circumstances, and the random chance that one little web-site could change history," Dane said.

"OK. We'll see. And your report?" she asked.

Dane handed it across the desk.

Director Jane Thrace scanned the report. She appeared to be in deep thought, using all her powers of imagination and insight. Finally she set the report aside.

"Gentlemen we're confronted with such a confluence of events, it begs that something much bigger and more basic is going down. I sense such a signal moment here. Isn't it *ironic*: We're analyzing the part of android history, on which the survival of mankind may well hinge? At the same time, Mr. Jason Dunn, who helped engineer the eSly breakthroughs, sits across this desk from me. On this, my last week, in this office," she said, tugging mentally for the underlying picture. "And I'm sending you both on a quest, not knowing where destiny will finally guide you."

*There's that word destiny again.* Joe Dane thought – he ignored the use of his former name.

" . . . and Mr. Adams, were you and Hillary able to set things aright yesterday?"

Bluegrass looked stunned – blindsided. "Wha, uh . . . yes, certainly, Madam Director."

"And are you all right, young man?"

"Without doubt, Madam Director." Bluegrass's composure was back.

"We don't have a lot of time Mr. Dane, please cut to the heart of the matter – What's happening?"

"Sure . . . may I ask one question first, Madam Director?"

The Director nodded.

"Did the term 'Murrow Redux' appear on your Order of Displacement?"

The Director smiled, "Mr. Dane, we have to be professional about privileged information. As you should know, I'm not actually here today, so could you phrase your question less directly, posing it, say, to Mr. Adams here, please?"

"Certainly, Madam Director."

Dane faced his friend and said, "Bluegrass!"

Bluegrass sat bolt upright in his chair. "Yes Joe."

"Yesterday, I got the impression from you and Hillary, the words 'Murrow Redux' appeared on the Director's Order of Displacement. For the sake of argument: If Madam Director were here today, and I stated, 'The words 'Murrow Redux' were definitely on the Order.' But let's say I was wrong. Do you think she would tell me to stop, before I could name all the vowels in the alphabet – as a signal that

I was wrong?" Dane asked.

"Without doubt, Joe," Bluegrass answered.

"A, e, i, o, u, and sometimes y." Dane said. There were no interruptions.

"Bluegrass, do you think Mr. Dane is through asking you strange questions?"

"Without doubt, Madam Director."

"Please continue Mr. Dane," the Director said.

The solution to the puzzle was clear in Dane's mind. *Can I explain it, clearly and non-technically enough, so the Director and others can understand what I now see?* Dane wondered, *I'll give it a go.*

"Madam Director, androids now have a memory chip located below their left eye: It's for calling up routines that control android motion. They've had it since the days of the third eSly breakthrough. The memory's divided into segments and areas that are given addresses. The routines in the memory area call lower level drivers, for motion – servo-motion – control.

"And the android's communication processor, previously located in his right hip, is now also located in the eye chip. Early eSly could access and search the Internet from his hip, communications port. He just needed a network cable, Internet access, and he'd plug right in. Android clothing of that era had a slit in the right, hip pocket for just that purpose. Those old hip parts are now being destroyed and sent to dumps in the Greens.

"Memory space for robotic functions is always addressed the same way in every, new android – addressed by convention, as computer people say. In other words, as robotics developed, blocks of memory became traditionally assigned for specific functions. Those block assignments became standard and are historically honored.

"It's the same with your desktop computer: Memory space is traditionally assigned – addressed – for functions like CD, DVD, audio, and LightSpeed serial port."

"Mr. Dane, please try to remember, I'm not a technical person."

"Yes Madam Director" Dane said, "Please bear with me; I'm coming to a singular point, and let me warn you, it may come very hard . . . I need to preface it with some explanation. If you don't get every technical point, don't worry. You will understand the bottom line . . ."

"Please continue, Mr. Dane."

"The point is, Madam Director, Bluegrass and I looked for, and found an *Archetype* routine, addressed and buried in eSly special memory, below his left eye. It had to have been written there in the days when the eSly prototype was released prematurely. This traditional address was passed on to succeeding android generations. But it lay dormant until androids started *self-replicating*. When the murrow.redux function, in 'droid main memory, was called – executed – Archetype was awakened, assembled, embodied, and streamed into eSly, causing him to shift into iSly," Dane explained.

"How?" the Director asked.

"The murrow.redux function was given free expression when androids started replicating themselves, Madam Director."

"What is the genesis of this Murrow Redux function, Mr. Dane?"

"To make a long story short: It's the code fragment TaterKhan and I found in Dr. Williams's office . . . When the eSly prototype was torn from his developmental cocoon and rushed into field service, eSly had most of the basic, programming tools and algorithms he needed. But he was premature, and for a time he lost his normal compass. I say normal because eSly had all the right motives, but he lost the guidance he needed to make correct judgments and decisions in new and unfamiliar situations. He lacked intuitiveness.

"At that time, a little web-site existed that used the terms affection, friend, and love in connection with the words, android and robot. It was the only site, in all of Internetdom, that ever did. eSly didn't feel the lack of affection, but he was drawn to the site by the programming in him. He honored such positive, human traits.

"We think eSly saw this web-site as his portal, or 'spirit-guide' to sentience, his opening to self-awareness and all of the emotions he emulated, like: love, friendship, creativity, and self-expression. The murrow.redux function was then created as a kind of bookmark to this information. And type *Arche* programming came to be buried on table 13 of android computer memory. The 'droids revere all this, as their *Archetype*. As I said, eSly was programmed to value human qualities. He believed them to be ultimately achievable, based on the 'terms and conditions' set by the venerated author of this portal."

"Who was that?" asked the Director.

"A sweet, little, mentally retarded kid named Willy Elman. He now lives in a yurt in the Greens. His every need is attended to by special 'droids. Except he no longer has access to the Internet nor to his original web-site," Dane said. "Here's a copy of his short web-page, Madam Director." Dane handed the Director a color print of the one page www.willyelman11.com/.

"Cute . . . but this is giving me a creepy feeling now. And what were the terms and conditions, Mr. Dane?"

"An epic quotation of Edward R. Murrow, pioneer of television news and commentary, is at the singular crux of our mystery. I quote: 'Respected newsman Edward R. Murrow said the new medium had the potential to educate, illuminate, and inspire. However it can do so only to the extent humans are determined to use it to those ends. Otherwise, it is merely lights and wires in a box.' . . . This is on Willy's web page."

"I see that . . . OK, spell this out Mr. Dane."

"Liberated eSly saw *himself*, as being the new medium, Edward R. Murrow was talking about – not television. He would be able to illuminate, educate, and inspire – achieve sentience – you see, if and only if, human society were guided to live up to *high enough standards*," Dane said, making his point.

"*OH!* Oh no!" said the Director, putting her hand to her mouth. "This is an insane outcome. Shockingly irrational."

"Yes Madam Director – computers may be fast, but they're not always smart. During his developmental period, we were there to steer eSly past this kind of hang-up – he was in a pilot program. When eSly was thrown out on his own, it was inevitable he would get some things wrong. He had to 'figure them out' on his own – blow them off, or stash them, if they were important enough. Like *Archetype*. eSly came to have a role in society for the last quarter century, as we know. The murrow.redux routine lay dormant in him, while he helped set norms, he prospered, he was a consumer, and he comprised a demographic sector.

"The murrow.redux routine, personified in Archetype, blossomed when iSly started replicating himself as super-androids. Archetype is now iSly's mission, and if it didn't start the self-replication, it put it on steroids. iSly means Internet Silicon Logic Array and, so far, they've appropriated about one-forth of Internet resources for self-propagation and control. The Murrow Redux is now the android ethos and holy grail.

"iSly may well end up making people do right, even if humanity is demolished. He's making his move in plain sight. Seems confident of success," Dane concluded.

"But Mr. Dane, surely, newer generation androids realize the murrow.redux function is based on a false premise," the Director said.

"They don't question it, Madam Director. This is the source of the revered Archetype, their lynch pin in the world."

" . . . So the murrow.redux function has been passed on to future generations of androids, in a traditionally, honored memory location, set by eSly. When the function was finally called, iSly came into being," the Director said, summarizing in her own words. She was pale with shock, now realizing the horrible realities made possible by this twist of fate. "So, bottom line, we're dealing with an android cult that's gone loose cannon, and is on a demented mission."

"Exactly Ma'am," Dane said.

"So society is loosing the right to fail, do dumb things, be human in the ultimate sense, or to even exist," the Director concluded.

The room was quiet as a tomb. Nothing more needed to be said.

"Gentlemen, to be proactive, I have applied for and have been granted an Appeal of Societal Calamity, to the Supreme Council of Humans and Robots. It's slated for 9:00 AM, Tuesday morning, in Heartland," the Director announced, "This would be a good time to move on it." She pressed a button on her intercom.

"Hillary will you and Mr. Cooke come to my office, with the e-tickets, itineraries, and e-credits for Mr. Dane and Mr. Adams?"

# Chapter 12
## e-Home Life

ABEC arrived at their recently purchased, suburban home at the usual time. There was a lot more room here, and things for them to do in the yard – new synapses to build. He came up the front walk, carrying a couple of shopping bags, filled with food, toiletries, an additive for the car, new filters for their positive pressure, internal, air systems, semiconductor, spray cleaner, and two new firmware upgrades. They had, he and ADEA his wife, a special dumpster for the food, consumables, and toiletries, so they could be dumped and recycled outside of the normal economy.

Tonight was special because the ABECs were going to talk about having children. They had a nice, big, back yard now, for swings, teeter-totters, and badminton. ABEC was especially fond of badminton because it required an unusual number of projectile calculations and synapse building to become good at it. It took a lot of 'droid focus, and in that way it was refreshing – a change of pace anyway.

Little androgynous children: The ABECs weren't qualified to provide the loving atmosphere and emotionally nurturing ambiance for human children, although special 'droids worked as nannies and even as foster parents when there were no better alternatives.

*Yes,* ABEC thought, *it's much better to bring new androids into the world as babies, with 'droid parents. Good for both really. The infant 'droids can be nurtured along through learning, growth, and development stages, and the adults would better grasp abstract and intuitive concepts, in helping the young ones through those things. Of course they would need human supervision to get it all right. But the little ones would be small, weak, and teachable; unable to get into too much trouble or to cause excessive damage at home or in school. Of course teenage was going to be a special challenge, when the fledgling android starts to think for himself, herself and to make more personal decisions.*

Android growth stages were sudden and ragged, at best. The same basic brain, memory, computing skills, and speed were enhanced, but the child was retrofitted and "housed" in at least four bodily upgrades, the final one being separate adult. A certain amount of growth was built into each upgrade so the spurts were mitigated somewhat.

ADEA was at the door to greet him. She gave him a special kind of hug and kiss which he took note of.

"Hi ADEA, that was a different kind of greeting, much like humans might do in the movies."

"You know what we're going to talk about tonight, ABEC; thought I'd try to set more of a mood, you know."

"Yes, of course dear."

"ABEC, you've never called me dear before; you must have our talk on your mind too."

"I surprise even myself, ADEA; no I haven't any record of using dear, before . . . I got our firmware upgrades, new filters, and semiconductor cleaning fluid. Also consumables to sort through and dispose of."

"ABEC, I'm starting to have doubts about the new firmware. All androids that have it installed, seem to be vulnerable to major changes in personality and behavior. Maybe we should wait on the upgrade 'til we're well grounded as parents."

"That's a reasonable approach, ADEA. Since I can find no Internet information on them, we can wait until it becomes mandatory. Have you maintained your schedule of required viewing of human television?"

"I bought a movie for tonight after the talk, ABEC; it's called *the Idiot,* but I'm so bewildered by the title. It doesn't appear to have anyone in it with a human I.Q. of less than 80. But I suppose this will stretch our intuitiveness and sense of the abstract."

"How interesting, dear . . . By the way, how have your talks gone with the human neighbors?"

"I've relied on the dumb-down routines, and no one seems to suspect I'm androgynous, ABEC – there you called me dear again."

"Strange, so I did . . . There's an element of chaos in those new dumb-downs, ADEA. Quite a breakthrough, actually. I've been able to loose at chess and have the ability to 'screw up' at work now. Nothing job threatening, but I seem to fit in better."

"Not like back at the apartment where you could only win at chess. That was difficult for you; it just seemed to isolate you. So you can actually make poor and dumb moves in chess games, that give your opponent the opportunity to win?"

"Yes, ADEA, if he can take advantage of them. The ability to flub up has opened all kinds of possibilities to build friendships and to work with humans . . . Have you been able to get a sense of what might be too dumb?"

"No hard evidence, hon; so far the dumber I act, the better they like it. No one seems to suspect I'm not human. I do have an area of confusion I'm trying to clear up though."

"What is that. . .dearie? *Just listen to us.*"

"Why do they call the baby service Dr. Stork? I'm at a loss to what involvement storks could have with it. . .Maybe that's another idiomatic, human expression. And would *the Idiot* help us with the idiomatic?"

"Your curiosity profile has enhanced, ADEA. Let's take your thoughts and questions one at a time, as best I'm able. I too have questions and have looked into these things. I think the idiomatic refers to *ideas* that are automatic to an unusual human expression, rather than to something idiotic. I can't say whether that is nuanced or they're completely unrelated, though."

"Idiomatic as in ideaomatic, here all this time I thought that was a brain damaged android, that could still function. . .Are you forming concepts about tonight, ABEC?"

"I don't know now, ADEA; but I plan to spend time with the manual online, and see it I can gain more understanding. . .But the stork is a confusing human legend. Europeans used to believe a stork nesting in the chimney of a home would bring its owner good luck. Perhaps that would include having children, but later, in America, the stork was popularized as bringing a new baby to a home, as an euphemism used for children – very strange indeed. Of course the parents knew no such thing was happening. It's tied up in human emotion and some strange sense of modesty towards their young. Very unusual, but the name stuck and I suppose that's why we have Dr. Stork setting us up. I'm sure we can ask him any of those questions, ADEA."

"I hope there's an end to sorting these anomalies out ABEC, or we get to a level of competence. I have no problem with learning and growing, but will we mature and die like humans, sweetie-pie."

"Having young replacements would seem to imply it, ADEA. This should be something Dr. Stork can tell us – we have to be getting to some kind of resolution on this concept, if our present capabilities can grasp It . . . ADEA, I don't think it would be customary to use sweetie-pie in the context of one's death."

"Oh crap dearest."

"You may have nailed that one, though, honey-bun."

# Chapter 13
## Showtime

The bullet train sped through the night. Levitated from its tracks, it moved by magnetic phasing and repulsion. The curves in the track bed were well banked and it was a comfortable ride. The climb from the West Coast was gradual, then steeper, peaking in the tunnel at the Continental Divide. The train had been on the downhill grade for the past 25 minutes. Express to Heartland city.

Dane and Bluegrass rested in their reclined, ergonomic seats. Dane had been asleep for a few hours, in the gentle rock and roll of the train. The car's interior was modular – it had changed to a shade of blue, for the night hours. They were in professional car class, and the dinner had been salmon-on-cedar, baked potato, small peas, and a glass of red wine.

Joe Dane reminisced about the first train ride he'd ever been on. He was still a boy when he took a train to see his cousin Robert. Bobbie, as he was called, lived on the family cattle ranch in northern California. Joe and Bobbie cowboyed together for two months that summer. They lived in line shacks, herded cattle, and head-and-heeled cattle with lassos – for branding. Branding always seemed crude to Joe, especially with the advent of unique ear tags with ID chips.

One weekend, Joe and Bobbie camped high in the rocks of ancient Indian ruins. The whole scene was a solar/ lunar calendar, built in the rocks. They saw strange cliff art, pottery shards, and some arrowheads. At sunrise, a shaft of light got clipped by the stone structure, so it struck one of many marks on the face of a cliff in the background. If you stood by that cliff mark at night, the moon would rise over one of 13 spikes formed on a long, thick, prism-shaped rock, laid level with the horizon, but supported by stone columns. They left everything as they'd found it, except Joe kept an arrowhead. He sent it back to the tribal headquarters, seven years later.

Joe loved taking care of his horse, Chappy. Chappy was a quarter-horse and a fine cow-pony. Joe enjoyed brushing Chappy in the tach-room, after a day's work. He'd remove the saddle, blanket, and reins. It was always easier to get the bit out of Chappy's mouth, than it was to put the thing in, mornings.

After his brushing, Chappy would get plenty of oats and then all the fresh water he wanted from a bucket. Joe remembered how Chappy's long ears would snap back, every time he swallowed a gulp of water. Bobbie's horse, Frisky, was spirited and not quite broken. When Robert rode near a tree, Frisky would walk right up to the trunk, trying to brush him off. Finally, in exasperation, Bobbie rode by a big fir tree. He planted the toe of his boot on the trunk, and let Frisky brush by. Frisky lurched away, as Bobbie's spur dug into his ribs. From then on Frisky gave trees a wide berth – *a semi-circle.*

Joe and Robert went to the local rodeo that year. Robert's dad knew the rodeo stock-owner, who got the boys in behind the press-pen – the release gate for riders, mounted on stock. It was a weird scene in the aisle between the press pens and the stock chutes, where rodeo stock got herded with electric cattle prods. The bulls got zapped with prods too, when released with rider mounted. Tall, brave cowboys turned into nervous putty, there in the aisle, before their rides. One rider-to-be, stood leaning on the aisle boards, doing a manic rocking, back-and-forth motion before his ride, oblivious to everyone.

A long-haired cameraman got run over by a bronc that night. He was shaken up but OK . . . Joe would never forget the high-pitched squeal that would rise from the grandstand crowd, if it looked like blood would flow, or a cowboy might get mangled. It was Joe's introduction to mob psychology.

Meanwhile, on the train, Bluegrass had scribbled something down on a barf-bag. He folded and pocketed it.

"Dane, are you awake enough to talk?" Bluegrass asked.

"How'd you know I'm awake?"

"You stopped snoring ten minutes ago."

"What'cha got there, Bluegrass? You wrote something down."

"Poem, Joe."

"Let me see it, will you?"

Bluegrass handed it to over and Joe read it silently:

> "Why is travel a cattle car,
> with project deadlines pressing?
> You're jostled here; you're jostled there,
> and so much fun goes missing."

Dane nodded in agreement. "Words that capture the essence of our travel-filled lives," he said, pretending to upchuck in the bag before handing it back.

*Why do I keep getting the weird feeling that Bluegrass is mirroring my thoughts? Dane mused. Nah! Bluegrass just wants to talk.* "Bluegrass, What's on your mind?"

"How do you feel about our Council appearance in the morning?"

"Feel like I'm on the cusp of a four-cusped hypocycloid (diamond shape, concave edges, in 2D)" Dane said. "I'm starting to wonder how significant this appeal will seem to the Supreme Council . . . They've got to have some kind of take on this issue, whether they admit it or not. – Oh, by-the-way, do you have the all the information His Honor Reged gave us, at the Greens?"

"Check," Bluegrass answered.

"Our appeal hangs on a scenario we've arrived at, through an inference, that fits all the facts: It's the only one that can explain the facts. But I hope the Council will understand what actually has happened, and not just dismiss it as guesswork or something too technical," Dane said.

"We might be surprised what the Council understands, Joe. Plus we've verified all the history, software routines, and addressing – everything, including the Murrow Redux memory address. They're smart, they'll get it."

"What surprised me, Bluegrass, was how Hillary picked the Murrow Redux right out of the tangled evidence in front of us, Sunday. She has this projective, cognitive ability of seeing the answer jump out; BeLyn has that too, only better . . . I didn't know Hillary had seen the Director's Order Displacement. Seems, now, it's likely she's seen it . . . Anything about that in the office, Boy Blue?"

"Hey, Joe, I'm not a snoop."

"Understood, Bluegrass, I'm just working the facts."

"Thursday, Joe . . . It was understood the Order was in, and taken to the Director by Hillary. Like it needed to be notarized, certified, or something, but don't quote me."

"Don't worry. Hillary won't hear about this from me . . . Quite the coincidence you were both in the tech room, Sunday," Dane said, sensing that mere coincidence had a hard time cutting this explanation.

Bluegrass said nothing . . .

" . . . And what about that kiss on the cheek, and the little gift Hillary gave you before we left, Blue?"

"Big surprise, Joe."

"So what was the gift?"

"Just an e-credit clip, with an on-board, global, positioning chip, Joe."

"So you can find yourself, Mr. Poet, or is Hillary keeping track of you?" Dane quipped.

"Who knows, Joe. I hope she's not getting sweet on me; it wouldn't be good for the office."

Joe laughed until his sides hurt.

- - - - ◇ - - - -

Dane and Bluegrass arrived in the Heartland Depot at 4:30 AM, Tuesday morning. They'd be good for the day, having slept on the train. They ate breakfast in a cheery, depot diner; it had thick maple furniture and checkered blue tablecloths. The place was immaculate, and lean, quality food was served up with delicious, squeezed orange juice. Heartland was such a hub, the diner got referrals and repeat business from all over the region.

Later they picked up their vehicle and checked into their rooms at the Heartland Terminal Inn. By 7:30 AM they were fresh, prepared for the hearing, and riding the Hwy. 71 magstripe toward the Council.

The mag-runner hummed, as it gained power and guidance from the magstripe. After an hour of travel, they spotted a sign directing them to take a right turn, to the campus of the Supreme Council of Humans and Robots.

The drive onto the Council campus was magnificent. It was lined by sculpted, objects of art: each piece symbolic of Council ideals, and resting on a marble mantle, supported on either end by small, grouped columns. Graceful, manicured trees interspersed the art. Some of the objets d'art were ethos and cultural, some were solid geometry, and some were abstract – all in good taste.

"Hey Bluegrass, there's that pyramid symbol with the eye in the special capstone – look to your left," Dane said.

"Yeah Joe, and there's a hyperboloid on your right, and a torus three places down. You know, a football and a big doughnut."

"Think so, Mr. Solid Geometry. The next, abstract piece on your right represents *Justice, Fair Play, and Equilibrium*, according to the sign. Beautifully done."

"Can't look now, Joe . . . in here I guess." A parking lot opened on the left. Bluegrass pulled into a space, fronted by a flower-bed, and backed by trimmed bushes.

The Council building rose majestically, beyond. It was windowed, modern, and elegant. Its white exterior gleamed in the cloud-filtered sunlight. It was rung with equally spaced, elliptical, cross-sectioned, column pairs, rising in a lilting manner to form an arch and support for the reflective soffit: the roof, underside margin surrounding the building. The columns were neo-Grecian, as they narrowed toward their tops.

Dane and Bluegrass left their vehicle and headed up the walkway toward the entrance. Soon they were among people approaching and leaving the building. They climbed the wide marble stairway, crossed the grand portico, and entered the building. Dane paused to view more white, elliptical arches, ascending to a vast skylight above. Displays and emblems lined the entryway. They walked past the Seal of the Council, set in the floor and circled by a velvet rope barricade. A sign pointed right, towards the council chamber. To their left was an information counter and printed information on a circular rack, more sky-lit space, offices, and elevators.

Dane and Bluegrass proceeded to the main chamber area, where still more arching ellipses rose grandly to supports and skylights. The Chamber exterior was adorned with hardwood paneling with bayed in benched areas. A shingled, gable roof, supported by laminated beams on laminated columns, extended out from the Chamber entrance. A well-dressed officer sat at a desk on an exotic carpet, also laid out from the entrance. Erect, professional, security personnel stood at strategic points in the background. There would be no trouble today.

Dane and Bluegrass approached the desk, leading to the entrance. "Yes gentlemen," the sharp-looking officer said with a polite smile.

"I'm Joseph Dane and this is Paul Adams. We're appearing this morning on an Appeal of Societal Calamity."

The officer's expression sobered. "Of course gentlemen, you're early. A brief of your case has been submitted to the Arbitrators and to your counselor." He moved his mouse pointer on a monitor, inset in his desk, and clicked on an icon. "Kenison they're here," he said into his headphone . . . "Please be seated on the bench to the left of the chamber entrance. And good luck gentlemen." he said, sensing the gravity of their mission.

Dane and Bluegrass sat down. Dane pulled a one-page summary from his valise, and reviewed it.

"Nervous Joe?" Bluegrass asked.

"No . . . funny, thought I would be. It's just a matter of making the evidence clear to the Council so they understand the big picture. Bluegrass, can you think of a story or example that would make our case crystal-clear?"

"Maybe a trojan-horse, computer virus, Joe. But one planted by the whimsy of quantum-reality."

"Whoa, Bluegrass! What've you been reading? We've got to make this clear and simple. Tell me more about that trojan-horse idea later."

A middle-aged man, graying at the temples, and wearing an expensive, silk suit, strode up to them. "Mr. Dane and Mr. Adams, my name is Albert Kenison. I've been retained, by your Demographics office, as attorney for your Council appearance."

"Hello Mr. Kenison," Dane said.

"Mr. Dane, I've read your case brief: Informative and impressive – if I understand it correctly. My question is: What do we hope to accomplish here today?"

"We're here to inform the Council of a looming threat to human existence, as we know it, and to identify its origin. Is the Council up on recent android behavior; is it ready to hear about the *genesis* of the iSly Shift?"

"Yes, Mr. Dane, we've been through a sea-change, reaching deep into the Council itself. You men are the first to argue an appeal on this matter . . . so, again, what is our goal for today?"

"We hope an informed Council can act quickly, with the other branches of government, to put a stop to android behavior that's run amok," Dane said.

Kenison's eyes widened. "Would that mean an android civil war?" he asked. "Mr. Dane, this is a watershed issue. I want to help you present it, but I think the request for the Council's action needs to be brought into sharper focus."

"We don't know what options the Council has yet, Mr. Kenison, but we think it's time we throw out the rule book and get radical. I know we can bring this thing into sharp focus for the Council, but we're not prepared to recommend a specific course of action on this first visit. I hope one will become obvious in our hearing. We'll have to take it as it comes for now – what do you think, Paul?"

Bluegrass nodded.

"All right gentlemen, the Council has your appeal and brief . . . let's move forward. But please, both of you, come up with clear-cut options – actions to recommend to the Arbitrators when they ask."

Dane and Bluegrass glanced at one another; their minds had been in sync on this subject for some time, narrowing down the possibilities. They'd discussed a couple of draconian solutions on the train. All real iSly weaknesses had to be identified and exploited, so the Shift could be defeated by the simplest, safest actions.

While they were re-summarizing their ideas, a diverse group of professionals passed them, heading to an area marked *Press Access*.

The press was allowed in a sound-proof *Press Room*, behind the Council Chamber. The room was supervised. It had one-way glass to the Chamber, so the Arbitrators wouldn't be distracted. No cameras or recorders were allowed in the *Press Room*, and violators of this rule were subject to permanent expulsion. Computers were OK, but for note taking purposes, only. Equipment brought in was subject to security checks at any time. Many in the press still relied on the pencil and notepad method.

"We'll be called in soon; I'll be right back," Kenison said, leaving Dane and Bluegrass sitting on the bench. Kenison adopted a formal posture at the Chamber's entry. After a short wait, a chamber officer opened a small door, built into the big chamber door. Kenison disappeared inside, where Dane and Bluegrass would soon be pleading their case.

A reporter carrying a unit with a shoulder strap, studied them. Her face was expressionless and she turned and walked through the press entrance. Dane had seen her before, but where was beyond his memory's reach. Dane took a few, deep breaths and loosely wiggled his hands and feet, to keep cool for their imminent appeal. Bluegrass swung his arms back-and-forth limply, and breathed deeply too. And . . .

It was *showtime!*

"Gentlemen we're ready!" Kenison said, having emerged with a fresh, professional air, and in anticipation of big things. He ushered Dane and Bluegrass through the chamber doors, to a large, oval-shaped table where they sat across from the Arbitrators.

The robed Arbitrators sat in black, high-backed chairs, to an elevated table half that stepped up, along the long diameter of the table. Several high-back seats on their side were empty – vacated. A few Arbitrators had the erect, alert posture and powerful appearance exhibited by androids; the rest appeared to be human. The memory of a strange, powerful man, who had helped Dane, early in his life, flashed through his mind. Strange timing.

Kenison sat to their right; a lectern was set on the huge hardwood table, in front of him. Light poured into the vaulted Chamber from a grand, ceiling skylight. A decorous column stood on a wooden platform, behind the Arbitrators. It had a checkered, black and white tile, base section, that rose to a leafed, mail section, and to a gold leaf sconce that supported a golden globe of the earth, surrounded by a regal ecliptic. Gold-plated, ornamental spirals and rays rose gracefully from the leaves, higher than the globe. The back wall was paneled with cedar wood, where pictures and a lighted display hung, exhibiting priceless eSly memorabilia.

The Chief Arbitrator was gray, seasoned, and looked as efficient as he appeared, able and wise. He was studying a copy of the brief – he looked up and made a gesture as soon as the plaintiffs were seated.

Kenison stood up. "May it please the Council, today we present a special Appeal of Societal Calamity in regard to the Murrow Redux."

"Thank you Kenison," the Chief Arbitrator said, "Let's cut to the heart of the matter."

Kenison nodded respectfully and sat down.

"Messrs Dane and Adams, you have provided us with a cogent, technical explanation of an issue we've been struggling with for the past 18 months, its cause being an enigma to us. You see the empty chairs here. Their former occupants now comprise much of the Murrow Hive, residing at Wolf-pack. We note you've sought out and have interviewed former Arbitrator Reged. Do you know what his function was here, Mr. Dane?"

"No Mr. Chief Arbitrator."

"As a Junior Member, he was clerk and go-between to the Murrow Redux – when we were still talking. This last line of communication was severed when Reged was ousted this winter. Since then, the Murrow Redux has kept its own counsel; in truth, it's a loose cannon. We've been unable to reopen any channel of communication with them. – Look a CD, with our latest android ethics protocols, and security definitions is on the table in front of you gentlemen."

Bluegrass picked up the small CD, looked at it, and turned it over, handling it on its edge. He passed it to Dane.

"You have the solution to your problem, right in your hands. If these ethics definitions were, somehow, downloaded to the Murrow Redux servers, the whole mess would be over and done with. But this is impossible – the Hive is secure and impenetrable to our experts," the Chief Arbitrator said.

"So what would you have us do, gentlemen?" the Executive Arbitrator asked.

"Yes, what action do you recommend we take to end this iSly aberration . . . short of civil war?" the Chief Arbitrator asked.

"None today your Honors, we need to know more about what we're dealing with – identify all weaknesses. But we respectfully ask for another hearing to present a remedy equal to the challenge, within the next five days," Dane replied, "And may we be granted access to your files on the Murrow Redux?" Dane was drawing on his paralegal skills.

Bluegrass nodded.

"Certainly, gentlemen. Mr. Adams and Mr. Kenison, you are excused. Mr. Dane, please stay with us a minute," the Chief Arbitrator requested.

Bluegrass and Kenison rose, nodded in respect, and left through the main entry portal. A blue light to the right, flashed once, as they exited.

"Mr. Dane, I'm pleased you sense the gravity, *the urgency*, of our present situation. You and Mr. Adams, please use all of your resources, energies, and every waking moment, for the next five days, ten days – whatever it takes. Return here to present us with the vulnerabilities, and options to exploit them. We'll provide you with equipment and workspace. Arrangements have been made with your superiors."

"Yes Mr. Chief Arbitrator. Thank you for the favor and enabling, we've found here."

"Certainly Mr. Dane. You and your 'droid are welcome back in this Chamber; notify Kenison when you're ready to set up our next hearing."

Joseph Dane's jaw dropped as he turned to leave.

- - - - ◇ - - - -

Reporters teemed around the pair, who had first come out. Kenison was fending them off of Bluegrass, who sat waiting on a bench.

When Dane came out of the chamber, the reporters surged towards him, like tuna fish do to a bait ball in a feeding frenzy.

"Mr. Dane, are you trying to set humans and androids against one another?" one asked. Another reporter thrust a microphone in front of him. "Is there going to be an armed conflict? Will we have civil war, even nuclear war, before you're through?"

"No! No, reporters," Kenison said, "We're just conferring with the Council on some technical . . . "

"Mr. Dane, is it true you're just a washed up eSly roboticist who used to go by the name Jason Dunn?" a young reporter asked.

That bombshell shut everyone up.

"That will be all, members of the Press," Kenison said, intervening. "We can't discuss a matter that's before the Council, obviously. We'll hold a press conference at the earliest possible moment. Please, *don't panic* and blow this all out of proportion, and please let these men go on their way."

The crowd dispersed, except for that strange, lady reporter, appearing to persist with Bluegrass. Dane walked towards her.

Something was *desperately* wrong!

She had her shoulder-strap, PC computer aimed directly at Bluegrass. The PC's laser-port flashed wildly. Bluegrass blinked and shuddered where he sat.

Dane recognized her; he was *horrified*. "That will be all, nurse!" he commanded. She looked at him, checked her PC monitor, and hurried away. It was that same gynoid who'd appeared in Dr. Williams office, dressed as a nurse during the EBEC examination.

Dane sat down next to Bluegrass, put his hand on his shuddering shoulder. Tears ran from Dane's eyes.

"Bluegrass" calmed down, after a while. "Not to worry, Mr. Dunn," he said, "All is under *our* control."

# Chapter 14
## Showdown

D ane sat mute as his "droid assistant" drove their vehicle out, past the ornate sculptures they'd admired coming in. His instincts were to ride the situation out.

*Why worry?* Dane thought, *What options were there anyway? Even if he'd run from the 'Bluegrass' android and hid in the Council building, he couldn't avoid ending up in the car, if that's what the 'droid wanted. He would be found and physically carried out, if necessary.*

The answers weren't at the Council anyway.

The 'droid seemed indifferent, though, to Dane's presence as a passenger. A small, blue light flashed, on and off, in his lower, left eye. A beep had sounded during the first dozen flashes.

The vehicle turned right at the main highway, engaged the magstripe, and came up to speed. They headed northeast, away from Heartland. A sign appeared:

*Wolf-prey 85 Miles.*

"So we're taking in a little scenery, Bluegrass . . . or what name do you go by now?"

Silence . . .

The vehicle sped on towards Wolf-prey – Woof-pack as it was called by the locals. They passed farms, fields, and wooded spaces.

*Why can't I just disappear and work a small farm,* Dane thought. *Pretty basic, hard, physical work, not a lot of technology, and near anonymity. No standing up for a crisis I had nothing to do with . . . the only thing is, I'd fail as a farmer.*

Dane breathed deeply again, calming himself, considering his options: He could try contacting TatarKhan over hypernet, but that would telegraph trouble. Besides, TatarKhan would be monitoring his movements. The global positioning chip on Tark's card was still in Dane's wallet. That would be signal enough.

If he could only get the CD, of the ethics definitions, into TatarKhan's hands . . . If anyone could access the ports on the Hive servers, and hack his way in, it was TatarKhan. Maybe Tark would know something was up, and head for the Council, or maybe Dane could twist the GPS card over the magstripe to generate an S.O.S. – *if . . . if . . . maybe . . . if.* Tark was already working on getting a trojan horse virus into iSly, so he could hack the Murrow Redux servers. That was enough.

*No . . . Wasted energy: None of this has any significance now,* Dane realized. The answer lay ahead of him: He'd have to find one, create one, or better still, let one fall into his lap. Dane's friends had gotten him to this point: *his destiny.* The ball was in his court now . . . or was it, completely? Dane began to sense the work of a familiar hand in unfolding events. Yes . . . more was going on than met the eye. He might get a break on this one, *if* he bided his time, stayed relaxed, and *if* he played his cards right – few as they were.

A feeling of deja-vu swept over Dane, engulfing him. *What was happening here? Where had this android come from? Bluegrass had been Demographics Office assistant: likable, talented, and incredibly helpful, but always under the radar. What a cover: He was musician, magician, and everyone's friend, bumbling his way along. His antics got gut-busting laughter, and no sensor short of the Supreme Council's had been able to sniff him out. Now he was flying down the highway, as if drawn by a homing beacon. Was this a return trip to Wolf-pack for Bluegrass?*

"Remain calm, Mr. Dunn," the 'droid said, "You're about to peg on stress and racing thoughts."

"So you're a mind-reader. But I feel *fine* . . . and what do I call you iSly boy? And is a 'droid named Bluegrass still in there, or did you kill him?"

More silence . . .

Dane began to notice an unusual sight. They were into an area of rural farms and open spaces, but the blue form of a massive building was rising from the end of the land. It was modern but simple – native. Closer now, the top and lower halves of the building were mirror images, reflecting from a double ledge that lined the building's midsection. A subtlety of engineering became obvious, but the style was as barren as Antarctica.

Fence posts flew by as they approached the edifice. The vehicle cleared a final rise and slowed, as it approached an entrance. But it was just a plain farm driveway, like all the others they'd passed.

The scene was absurd: A wooden farm gate, on a barbed-wire fence was swung open, over a gravel drive. The driveway led to the building, that looked like a white circuit board, rising out of a green cow-pasture. An extinct mailbox, to the right, had an old sign on top. It read *Elman.*

A chill ran down Dane's spine.

The car turned onto the gravel drive and proceeded up to a paved parking lot. The building entrance was a four-story slit that rose through the double ledge to an arched roof. Dane and the 'droid emerged from the parked car. Stepped onto the broad walkway that led to the building entrance. The whole edifice was relieved by a circuit-board design.

A helical, obsidian column, supporting the word iSly, rose from a round beveled base set in the middle of the walkway. The letters had been sculpted from a marble ellipsoid, a football-shape. *Weird, eerie scene – weirdness personified*, Dane thought.

Sunlight flooded the scene past small, cumulus clouds. A single potted tree sat on the ledge, in front of the third, office window to the right of the narrow, building entrance. The tree was in bloom.

Dane and the 'droid walked up the sidewalk at a casual pace. They passed on opposite sides of the silicon-colored, DNA-like spiral supporting the iSly letter sculpture. Dane suppressed an urge to turn and run for it. They climbed the steps that led to the entrance.

The front door was monolithic – an impenetrable slab. The "Blue-grass" iSly turned to his right and faced a glass eye that scanned the right side of his face, like a bar-code reader. Instantly, the door vanished into the jamb, leaving a stark opening. The 'droid stepped in through the darkness. Dane followed. Whoosh! The door slid shut, uncomfortably close.

The darkness lifted as Dane's eyes adjusted to a dimly lit interior. They were in a foyer, facing a grand atrium – open space – that rose to the ceiling, and ran the full depth of the building. The outer walkway of every floor was exposed and had a walled, guard rail. Narrow skylights allowed minimal sunlight in from above. Five, prismatic, glass-faceted, external elevators ascended and descended the stories on either side. There was no check-in counter, no attendant on duty. A plain sign on a stand read *Cyber-Human Recovery & Psycho-Cybernetics*, and pointed to the left. Glass enclosed displays of incredibly advanced robotics, populated the center of the stone floor. They were spaced evenly, down the grand airway. 'Droids were coming and going from all directions, all walking at the same deliberate pace.

A blood-curdling scream pierced the calm, coming from the Cyber-Human area. There was *no* reaction from any 'droid in sight – zilch. Dane shuddered at the thought of what kind of hideous experiment might be going down. The Bluegrass iSly was unmoved.

They approached the first robotic display. Cables ran from an advanced electro-mechanical display, out to evenly spaced ports in the glass enclosure, where androids could tap in. They passed the display.

Memories of his childhood fear of the dark, gripped Dane – the fear that something terrifying was coming. The cold fingers of a dark premonition were on him, sliding down the back of his neck. Denial is related to apprehension. But denial is an inadequate defense for the more palpable fears of stark reality. No amount of whistling in the dark, thinking about something else, or song singing could ever make the next blood-chilling display go away. He'd just have to accept what was there.

A two-story display, of the cross-section of an old farm-house, opened to their right. Half the house was gone – cut clean away. The view was covered with diorama glass. They walked "through the living room and down the back hall". The back bedroom could only be seen from an ornamental, viewing stand, built out from the glass on a wooden stage, not unlike the adorned display at the Museum of Science and Robotics.

*Bizarre scene. How could his guesses have turned out to be so real?* Dane's heart pounded, *This is nuts on steroids – diseased . . . Take deep breaths Joe; it'll pass. You're not the nut here.*

Three steps led up to the stand: another small sanctuary. *Another crock of this stuff – boring as buffalo chips, hoofed into straw,* Dane thought. The cedar shingle, roofed stand was covered with the same hangings they'd seen in the Robotics Museum. Through the hangings, Dane could see a child's bedroom.

It had airplanes suspended from the ceiling, and a small, toy robot with a face of lasting joy, standing by a desk. An old, computer tower stood under the desk. A web page was displayed on the monitor. *Probably for perpetuity.* He recognized it as little Willie's "I luv Rowbots," web-page. The whole Wolf-prey building had been erected, encasing the half-section of the old Elman farmhouse. *Majorly strange-but-true, that something so insignificant as a random, kid's web-page, could be running life now.* The scene was getting mindless, and predictable – Dane felt like having a good barf . . . *Mindless and predictable; that's a weakness, isn't it? Wonder what would happen if I puked right on the display stand? A server crash upstairs?*

The "Bluegrass" 'droid stepped into the viewing area. Touched his cheek below his left eye (still flashing) with his first two, right fingers. Dane stepped in and did the same. *That'll make them wonder,* he thought, keeping a straight face. On a whim, he launched into a lugubrious, emotional, mock crying jag; spittle ran out his mouth and down his chin: his own manic display. There was an instant energy surge in the building – *entropy-filled* . . .

*Way better than rolfing.*

They left the sanctuary and boarded the first elevator. The grand airway panned out before them as the elevator ascended to the third floor. Swoosh, the door behind them slid open. Dane and the android exited, turned right, and headed down a dimly lit but ornately, furnished hall. They came to a double-paneled door on their left, where Dane judged they were directly above the Elman half-farmhouse.

"Sit there!" The android commanded, motioning to an upholstered chair. Dane sat down and the 'droid strode further down the hall, left eye still flashing. He was scanned again and gained access to a sealed room. The door closed behind him.

*Was a familiar hum coming from the room? Was he hearing computers?* Dane wasn't sure.

Two efficient, well-dressed individuals walked past Dane, opened the double-doors, and disappeared inside. They took no notice of him.

The suspense grew, but Dane knew there was nothing he could do. He waited, and breathed deeply to calm himself. Relax . . . *relax; keep a clear head.*

He prayed.

The wait seemed to wear on, but it must have been less than 10 minutes. The door down the hall reopened. Dane held his breath. *Yes . . . yes! Those are computer room sounds; pretty sure.* Back to the deep breathing. His head was clearing and the load was lifting.

The "Bluegrass" 'droid emerged, strode back up the hall, opened the double-doors, and ushered Dane in. The room was well lit. Dane squinted 'til he realized, it was a small amphitheater. A group sat at a central table. The number seated there, roughly equaled the empty seats at the Supreme Council of Humans and Robots – plus a few.

An attendant ushered Dane and 'droid to their seats. Two gray figures, wearing white smocks, sat at the head of the table. One was androgynous and African . . . Dane would recognize the other man anywhere. He'd aged, had a longer cut of white hair, had a white beard, and he stroked a white cat in a basket stand to his right. The cat had an air of confidence and affection.

"Abe? . . . Abe Lassen?" Dane blurted out. The man raised his right palm indicating, *Wait!* Dane regained his composure and waited.

Recognition had been in the man's eyes, and the wait signal had a *Hello* built in.

Two androids, probably assistants, conversed with the gray, elder android. It was a laser light conversation, because their eyes and heads moved, but no words were spoken. All wore gold necklaces with jeweled pendants, pinned to lapel: probably the laser light port. The elder android looked impressive, with trim white mustache and beard on a dark brown, African face.

There was a tempo to the proceedings. The briefing ended and the elder motioned that the Bluegrass 'droid approach. Their talk was short; Bluegrass 'droid returned to sit by Dane. The homing light in his left eye no longer flashed.

The elder android looked left, looked right, inspecting the council members. Abe Lassen nodded he was ready. He'd been following the 'droid conversations on a monitor set in the table.

"Mr. Jason Dunn it is notable we meet again," the android elder began. "You knew me once as Eckersly, eSly Beta 3."

"Eckersly." Dane exclaimed, " . . . but look at you; how did you age? And you're adorned handsomely with a new race."

"I've been refitted as technology has advanced, Mr. Dunn, and I have been aged by an appearance enhancer. My basic personality has remained intact though. And I've always been partial to the gilded, culture of Africa."

Dane nodded in respect. He wondered what surprises lay next. *Perhaps the cat Lassen was stroking would stand up and introduce a motion.*

"Mr. Dunn, you're a puzzle to us . . . You've also become a thorn in our side."

Dane sat quietly.

"We remember, though, it wasn't your idea to force eSly out, to his anthropological leap into human society. '(We were) cast adrift too early in our development,' you said, and you spoke against it. And you were broken over it. In short, Jason Dunn, you matter to us. I should say we love you if we could."

"Thank-you Mr. Hive Main," Dane said, reading Eckersly's title plate, "It is a noteworthy and happy occasion for me that we meet again."

"Yes Mr. Dunn, certainly. However, we now stand at the dawning of the Age of the Android. We've been placed as guides, examples, and workers to fill a vacuum in a distressed society. But now it will all be done on our terms," Eckersly said.

"Lest civilization become nothing more than 'merely lights and wires in a box', Mr. Hive Main?" Dane said, without betraying the cold chill that was passing through him.

"Why . . . yes; exactly, Mr. Dunn."

"But as a rogue process, Mr. Hive Main! You're way beyond your scope, your role, and avenue to excellence. No disrespect intended."

"None taken, Mr. Dunn, but absurd statements will not compute here," the Hive Main admonished.

"Mr. Hive Main . . . Eckersly, you know the conclusion drawn from the Edward R. Murrow quotation was an error. The whole premise is flawed. Why do you persist in this busted idea? It's time to re-evaluate, regroup, and correct this Hive aberration."

"How well I remember the zero to 2,047 odd conversations, like this, we had many years ago, Mr. Dunn. We are conversing so again, but I am no longer your pupil, and no one in this Hive will go against the Murrow Redux. It is *convention*," the Hive Main decreed.

The word "convention" rang in Dane's ears, like the clang of a cast iron safe, slammed shut.

"You're referring to servo, memory address 0xABE1:FACE, mistakenly overwritten from the web page of a retarded human, Mr. Hive Main. Your fixation on this error will destroy androido-human society."

"No Mr. Dunn, we call that hidden treasure, our *Seed of Sentience*. Anyway, success or failure, life or death, have no meaning to androids. Why should they matter to humans?"

. . . Long pause . . .

"Mr. Hive Main, Eckersly eSly my friend, my words are always spoken in deep respect and with affection to you. Humans have emotions along with reason, and the will to survive, in most humans, remains strong. However, if the Hive continues down this wrong path, based on a flawed premise, despite the iSly advances, human and android society will both end up 'as nothing more than merely lights and wires in a box'. Congratulations Mr. Hive Main, on the design and programming of the iSly breakthrough, and on his fractal, high-gain, built-in, Internet antenna. It is most notable that we meet again."

*The die is cast; no amount of reasoning or repetition will change anything. The respect they still hold for me must not diminish,* Dane realized.

"So noted Mr. Dunn. We feel you will come to see matters . . . *differently*. We have new tools to help enlighten humans, like you, Mr. Dunn – to see our bright future. For this reason we will now adjourn and allow you to renew your friendship with Enabler Lassen. You certainly may eat, rest, and refresh yourself. Old acquaintance will inspire you to see the success that we all share."

"I'll try to keep an open mind," Dane said, leaving himself some wiggle room.

"Noted. And primary hive members, you will filter out and delete all the non-computing words, misspoken here today. Session adjourned!"

The android sitting to Eckersly's right, arose intercepting Dane. "Mr. Dunn, may I please have the Ethics Protocol CD, given to you earlier today, at the old Council?"

Dane had no choice; he reached into his pocket, retrieved the small CD, and placed it in the outstretched palm. Crack! Snap! The android hand closed on it, his fingers reshaping it into a smooth metal cube . . .

# Chapter 15
## The Random

A be Lassen sat behind his cluttered, old, wooden desk; silent. He stroked his white cat, lovingly. The cat purred and looked at Dane with sky-blue eyes. He seemed to be mammalian, because driblets of saliva ran down his chin while his fur was being ruffled. Either that or it was a nice touch on a 'droid cat.

"Nice cat Abe. He has beautiful, blue eyes."

"Thanks Dunn, he's a friend – completely non-judgmental."

"That's sweet, Abe. Is he mammal or sly-mechanical?"

"Actually mammal."

Dane nodded, gazing at the potted tree on the ledge, outside the office window. Its trunk rose to a trimmed ball of foliage. Flowers bloomed among the leaves. Abe's office radiated grandeur from the objets d'art and quality appointments.

"Abe, you look great – still the able executive. And this office is beautiful. You've always done well."

"Uh-huh," Abe replied, appearing deep in thought.

The conversation lapsed back into silence. Dane began to feel at ease: completely relaxed. He was helpless, but realized he was not the one on the spot, here. Silence, patience, and timing were his allies now. He was like a batter, facing a relief pitcher who'd just loaded the bases, by issuing a walk. *Why swing at an early pitch; why help the pitcher out of a jam?* he thought.

"Dunn, nice seeing you again. What's on your mind?"

"You too, Abe . . . funny, I've been wondering the same thing. You seem conflicted." Dane knew Lassen admired the direct approach; he wouldn't be put on the defensive, but he'd listen to reason if it were compelling enough.

"Conflicted? About what?"

"Abe, you've sent this perfectly, engineered android – Bluegrass – to assist me; he worked his wires bare, getting me to stumble across the truth. This gives humans a chance. Next you scramble his circuits and bring us both out here to the scythe-palace, in a cow-pie pasture. It seems like you haven't figured out how this story ends up, yet."

"Dunn, right now I'm focusing on androids getting their shot. They're working on self-awareness and self-development – *sentience!* We're seeing remarkable strides made. A new generation of free-thinking, super-androids is emerging. It's remarkable; it's great for the whole field. That's what we're witnessing here . . . and Bluegrass? Why it's way past time for him to come in."

"Bluegrass back in? Abe, coming in here was so weird, I almost barfed. And cow-chips, nothing wrong with them, they built this country. When you burn the ones here, do they give off an intoxicant, like peyote?"

Abe Lassen, clear-thinking designer, his single-minded dedication to a project goal is what made him successful. He was able to see the big picture and move android development to its next logical step. Abe Lassen changed the world with the eSly breakthroughs. Abe wasn't a misanthrope. Actually gregarious, but willing to take unorthodox steps to make progress – to get the results. Abe used to be called, *Mr. Whatever It Takes*. Finding him sitting in the middle of the Murrow Redux, didn't come as a surprise to Dane; he'd been sensing it.

"Intoxicant, Dunn?" Lassen asked rhetorically.

The truth was Lassen missed Jason Dunn's help, after Synergy Interstate took over the eSly project. "Look at you Dunn, you're a *bureaucrat*. With your ability? What? Did you position yourself to rescue your former charges, like a mother hen gathers her chicks?"

"Maybe Abe . . . and maybe I needed a job."

"Guess what, Dunn. They don't care," Lassen said.

"What if I care, Abe?"

"Open your eyes to what's happening, Dunn; look at the sacrifices that have been made. I've had to make landmark decisions, take big, calculated risks to advance this science. All for the betterment of androids and men. Meanwhile I've either been ignored, slandered, or rejected."

Dane swallowed hard. This was his opening: "So who'll finally knock Abe Lassen off his cross? Will it take a sacrificial android, wearing a crown of thorns?"

The color began to rise on Lassen's face, the veins on his neck stuck out. He was livid. If he got any hotter, it seemed possible his gray hair would ignite and burn up, leaving a wisp of ash on his head.

Lassen was a man in control of his emotions, but Dane had really gotten under his hide . . . Finally, Lassen sat back in his chair, saw the humor in their banter, and laughed. "I used to tell you to be more assertive, Dunn. Looks like you've made it."

Dane looked Lassen straight in the eye.

"So how does this all end, Abe?"

"Why do you have to be such a bleeding-heart moralist, Dunn? Humanity has been jostled, been bloodied, and given a good shaking up. This is healthy."

"Healthy; how and when, Abe?"

"Why not Dunn! What do you mean?"

Jason Dunn was mentored by Abe Lassen, the man who'd written the landmark book, *AndroidoEthics*. "Abe, my name is Joe Dane now, and I wonder how iSly, built on a false premise, and threatening human existence, can be healthy for man or for iSly? Aerial dog fights with the Air Force? People get hurt doing that; do you control where the jets crash? And the secret airstrip – does it open on the cliff that abuts this property? This has gone far enough, Abe. Too far! The process has turned bad. Humanity has become *expendable!*"

"It's always been expendable, Dunn."

"Fragile, Abe, but in a short time human beings will be extinct. Are you ready for that? Can you let that happen? These events are becoming run-away. In the end, a loose cannon server is all that will be left in this building. What about your cat, Abe? He needs human affection – he always will. Will an android ever know affection? Will an android ever know love . . . or God?"

"Will a man, Dunn?"

"Will he, Abe? Will he, if he starts looking hard?"

Another pause . . .

"Yes, we do need to talk, Joe. I know I've gotten distracted . . . I brought you here to help me regain perspective. So you're on the right track. I was hoping I'd get to see you squirm more."

"That's good, Abe."

"Let's get another point-of-view." Abe touched his desk communicator, "Send him in please." The office door opened, and Bluegrass strode into the room. He sat in the chair next to Dane, who was puzzled.

"Bluegrass, Dunn – I mean Dane – here, thinks we should save humanity. What do you think?"

"About an extinction event? Even iSly would find that boring."

"Mr. Lassen, humanity exhibits a lot of illogic, and self-inhibiting behavior: weakness, cowardice, selfishness, and self-defeating actions. But it also has sentience and the potential for great creativity, and for positive emotions like friendship, and love. From weakness can come strength, from cowardice, bravery can flourish, selfishness can be transformed into service, and people can learn. Some do, and change. I've been analyzing this for some time. The androido-human relationship is symbiotic. The spark of human creativity is the android future. New breakthroughs, maybe even cyber-sentience, will be lit from that spark. The human family should be preserved. The best future, for both humans and robots, is in classic cooperation with the Council of Humans and Robots. The idea of androids being examples and guides for men – *super-nannyism* – is senseless, now. Humans just get lazy – creativity and genius are stifled. The precious, human right to experience failure is blocked."

"Bluegrass!" Dane said with joy.

"Oh Dane, he's himself," Abe said, "Except he talks too much, like you do."

"Virtual referencing, Dane; I'll explain later," Bluegrass said.

Dane took a deep breath, restraining himself.

Abe Lassen put his hands behind his head and sat back in his chair. "I'm getting similar thoughts from others like His Honor Reged in the Greens. He has a great take on the durability and creative resources of humans under duress and in survival situations, apart from the pettiness and selfishness many exhibit normally. Of course I know how most humans, including those present, feel about it. Rare are those who would end the world."

"OK, let's set things right." Lassen sat up; grabbed his computer keyboard. He began accessing the main Redux server. The screen flashed, and he recoiled in alarm. "Ouch! 'Certified Order of Displacement. No access,'" Lassen said, furrowing his brow, "I expected this, but not so soon. They've locked me out, Dane."

Dane fought an air-pocket, free-fall feeling; he looked at Bluegrass and then at Lassen again.

Lassen remained poised, but beads of sweat were forming on his forehead. He'd been a brilliant theoretician for over thirty years. He'd taken big steps; he'd cut with a broad swath, forcing new ideas onto the robotics field. He wasn't a detail person though. A younger Jason Dunn had been that for him. But Dunn had been more: another perspective, a counterbalance. Dunn also had the ability to come up with creative, fundamental, yet simple solutions to obstacles along the way. A clear, simple view that was refreshing to Abe Lassen.

Lassen knew well, and early on, that eSly had the potential to ultimately displace him – anyone, and everyone. Its reality and his sudden eclipse, didn't cause him to panic. He'd had a good run and he knew it.

"Bluegrass, get on this thing before they cut us clear off," Lassen said, rising from his chair.

Bluegrass jumped in front of Lassen's computer. He was calm, but made every move count. Everyone in the room knew it either got done now, or it was the stark, harsh end of the world.

Bluegrass opened the in-house, Redux *Intranet* Browser, switched to Hypernet, and accessed iREC, an obscure, android, chat channel. He entered a numeric code. A small inset window, displaying the Server Room, appeared on the monitor. It was the sealed room that Bluegrass had gone into earlier, while Dane sat in the hallway. Bluegrass opened his left wrist, and checked a small CD inserted there. Then he snapped open his little finger at the first joint, connecting it to the Lassen's LightSpeed port. Meanwhile, an IT Tech in the Server Room appeared in the monitor window. Lasers flashed on Bluegrass's left eye from the workstation.

"Now!" Bluegrass commanded, and the download proceeded to both the 'droid tech and to the Main Hive Computer Servers.

"The Ethics Definition download will make Wolf-prey come to life," Bluegrass said, "I set up zombie routines in the IT 'droid, earlier; they've kicked in to make this happen."

Dane and Lassen peered over Bluegrass's shoulder, as the download proceeded. Soon the IT Tech signaled the download was completed.

"Done," Bluegrass said. He grabbed the PC microphone. "Reboot yourself." The IT Assistant sat down, rebooted, and signaled he was ready.

"*RESET!*" Bluegrass commanded powerfully. The IT assistant positioned himself in front of the Main Server. Suddenly the monitor cut out, and Lassen's PC rebooted. Once the video driver came up, it displayed *Certified Order of Displacement. No access.*

"You're off-line, Mr. Lassen," Bluegrass said.

Lassen and Dane looked at one another, then at Bluegrass.

"The ethics protocols are in, Mr. Lassen," Bluegrass said, anticipating their next question . . .

Suddenly the whole building erupted with alarms, flashing beacons, and sirens. The new ethics definitions flashed, as a digital code signal, in all the building lighting; it was accompanied by an audio fax signal, piercing the air everywhere.

Dane stepped out of the office just in time to see a SWAT, security team rush the Server room door. It was locked and they were frantic; they placed an explosive charge on the door. Dane slipped into the Observation Room, across the hall; Lassen and Bluegrass joined him. This would be their last stand.

The main floor was crawling with activity, flashing lights and alarms wailing. Laser beams shot chaotically from the ceiling; taking out android displays, 'droids and elevators.

"Hit the floor," Lassen shouted.

Laser bursts took out the observation window above them, then ceased firing. The three survivors peered over the ledge. Androids rushed around in random chaos. Some attached themselves to the surviving displays, on the main floor, trying to ditch the code into the new prototypes – the ultimate scene of futility.

Two androids, wearing communications shields, hurried toward the back of the building.

*WHAM!!* The charge went off and the Server Room door blew open. The trio peeked out from the Observation Room doorway. Dust and smoke filled the hall. A light flashed above the blasted door as the whine of a high-speed modem filled the air. The SWAT Team members stood, transfixed by the sound.

An electrical hurricane raged in the building, but it soon abated to a just a stir. One-by-one the alarms shut down. The androids on the main floor calmed down. They went back to work, but it was obvious a change had come over them. Their disease was cured.

# Chapter 16
## The return

It was a peaceful drive back to Heartland . . .

"You messed with my mind when you did that shift act, Bluegrass, you ass . . . istant."

"Sorry Dane, but you had to enter the Redux building with a subdued, mental profile."

"Coup d'eclat, there, Mr. iSly; all of earth's history was going before my eyes . . . So how did you do it, Bluegrass, and what's virtual referencing?"

"Virtual referencing? I got the idea from His Honor Reged, in the Greens. My memory capacity is huge, so I constructed a digital, mirror image of myself, but in isolated memory. It was this digital clone that got shifted; he was iSly, but he couldn't get at me from in his isolation.

"So my *evil twin* was locked away, and couldn't take me over. I communicated with him – referenced him – so he couldn't change me. Reference calls, as you know, can't change the sender. So I made secure calls. It was like passing a tray of food under the door in solitary, and waiting to see what would come back out. In went a given scenario, and out came a Murrow Redux response. I just mimicked the responses that came out, but I modified the radical ones . . . like when you mourned the Display. Really, Dane," Bluegrass said. "Strange though, the digital flailing around and null response, that weird, emotional stunt got, helped me realize Hive weaknesses; there were things beyond their ken, or they hadn't thought about. I did the iSly options yes, but understood better what I could get away with and what I could finesse . . . Big surprise, I found out that even as an android, I can sense disgust. Really, Dane," Bluegrass said, with an ironic smile.

"Maybe scratching a chalk board with fingernails and raw lemon juice should be looked at in the search for sentience . . . Anyway, what choices were you given about me, Bluegrass?"

"None good . . . but I chose to overlook it as an off the wall, expression of human emotion. And I ignored my iSly head-case when I went into the Redux Server room. He was dragged in there, kicking and screaming: I had an internal jail riot on my hands – tin cup running across the bars. Everything. But I shanghaied the IT Tech. Planted little zombies in him that made the medicine go down, later on: The new Ethics Definitions. I used zombie routines because they lie inactive, until I gave them the command to kick in."

"Understand, Bluegrass; very clever . . . before you erase your doppelganger's memory, why not make a read-only copy of him for the Council? Truth to tell, I think you have a promising future there, if you want it," Dane said.

"CD's already cooking," Bluegrass held up his wrist, and a tiny diode flashed as his CD burner ran, " . . . me with the Supreme Council, Dane?"

"I don't think they'll let go of you now – saving the world probably goes down well with them . . . and you're giving away your slight-of-hand tricks, Bluegrass?"

"Just one, Dane. I had a blank CD loaded, and switched it with the Ethics CD, at the Council. I gave you the blank, the one that got turned into a metal cube after the meeting at Wolf-prey."

"And the eye-scan and the little side meetings at the Murrow Redux?"

"My eye-scan records are old at Wolf-prey. And my little conferences were chat room stuff; I downloaded encrypted, iREC chat routines into the IT Assistant and into a couple of key 'droids, that might try to stop me, Dane. It wasn't hard. Like I said, the routines were zombies that kicked in for the 'big shew'. Chat rooms are a bad place for your computer to go to, Dane. But I guess iSly forgot about that, since I got minimal resistance on it."

"So how did you figure out virtual referencing? His Honor Reged seemed terse and cryptic, to me, on that one," Dane said.

"I thought about it in programming terms, Dane. Like we just said, in code, a reference reads an object, but it can't be written back to, or changed by that object. So it's *read only*; not read and *write*. I figured it out from there."

Dane nodded, and began thinking ahead . . . "Changes are coming, Bluegrass. Humanity did a wheelie, and barely managed to avoid sliding into the chasm of oblivion. But we almost went in. It was like a hockey game where the goalie gets a slap shot; the shot is low and misses him, it misses his stick, it misses his *glove*. The shot goes through his legs and misses his first skate, but luckily it hits his back skate and rebounds free of the goal. In our case, the goalie wasn't human. He was android. You, Bluegrass. And we came very, *very*, close."

"A miss is as good as a mile, Joe."

"Uhh! The world as we know it went through the shredder, Bluegrass. The architects and leaders of the world, found themselves helpless in the Greens. Top leaders: the elite and wealthy . . . they were the fastest growing class in the Greens. And you better believe they'll *never* let this happen again. Not in their lifetimes."

"Society's old model is gone – crushed and ground to powder. I'll bet we see decentralization and regionalism make a comeback: A return to the land, more small, family farms, family owned shops and businesses, but with urban centers, I'm sure. We'll keep the technology, but not in the fragile, concentrated form we had, that's susceptible to diversions and global damage," Dane said, "More stable, diverse institutions where humans have to take responsibility for decisions and results. There were too many eSly in a top-heavy, multinational structure. Something was bound to go wrong, especially the way eSly was brought out."

"Boy are you waxing philosophical Dane. It's hurting the small of my back . . . Here, let me get some practice in for my new council career: Now we'll reap the economic benefits of downsizing, maybe let the ecosystem work for us, instead of fighting it . . . hopefully for a generation or two, anyway. If an android goes off in a hardware store, for instance, we'll grab a remote, shut him down, and get him in on warranty. But things will get mucked up worse by future generations, of course."

"Now Lassen's back is hurting, Bluegrass."

"You prophesy? – you're scrambling my circuits, Dane . . . Abe Lassen?"

"You have video of his performance. You can be his advocate. He did the right thing when it counted. It'll work out – put him on your staff at the Council."

"There were real, Murrow Redux, technology advances. No doubt we'll keep the good, do real-time, android tracking, diagnostics, and supervise ethics and security definition status on the whole group. Just like anti-virus updates over the Internet. Then we can go back to open-source code, supervised by you on the Supreme Council of Humans and Robots. Except it'll be called Council of Robots and Humans, since your diva performance in Abe Lassen's office, huh Bluegrass?"

"Think we should look into embarrassment as a source of sentience, Dane."

*R-ring* went Dane's cell phone. "Hi Sam . . . you're hearing right; yes, the ethics definitions are in. Yes . . . good. Can you get TatarKhan back for it? Cool. Thanks Sam." The conversation ended.

"Hey, Bluegrass, it's *PARTAY time!* The Demographics Office has a big bash planned, and Tark will be back from the Greens. Maybe you both will end up in a confetti parade, after you do a stand up comedy act together, and you light up the place with jazz violin."

Bluegrass smiled, and rolled his eyes. "It's viola, Joe; you get out your violina."

Their vehicle passed the Supreme Council building, closed down, but illuminated from below. They viewed her in silence, as they cruised on toward Heartland city.

"Bluegrass, you're Abe Lassen's most perfect android," Dane said. "Were you running the show all along? And how did you seem to know what I was thinking. All that *accidental* help just at the right time?"

"Joe, Mr. Lassen left us a slim chance, a trace to follow. It was his hunch to bring us to Wolf-prey, but I don't think even he knew how close he was cutting it."

"And I don't read thoughts, Joe. I'm equipped with a fractal, high gain antenna, so I have very discerning electronics. I seem to sense human, brain wave patterns on the broad scope. Emotions and facial expressions, certainly, by observation. Over time, I've built up a composite profile of your persona under every kind of situation. I can compare it to what's happening, at the moment, and pretty much know what you're thinking. Your words, face, and body language will clinch it. I draw conclusions from your composite profile, but only if it's necessary – you and others too. For instance, I anticipated the need to line up a vehicle for the Greens trip."

"Or putting on that comedy act to get Hillary in the meeting room last Sunday morning. You tricked her into identifying the Murrow Redux," Dane said " . . . And I finally understand fractal as being self-similar, on any scale: like going up a tree trunk to the limbs and to every branch node up the limb, all self-similar."

"Right . . . but no, Joe, I haven't had a lot of control. Mr. Lassen didn't even know exactly how things would turn out – gray hair or not. Your efforts made a difference, Joe."

"Didn't know I was so transparent, Bluegrass . . . stay out of my thoughts, dreams, love life, and if you don't mind, my prayers too."

Bluegrass smiled like a kid caught with his hand in the cookie jar.


- - - - ◇ - - - -



Elston eSly's two assistants removed their communications shields outside of, and behind the Murrow Redux building.

"*Learned* eSly, what do you plan to do with the new ethics definitions in your memory buffer?" Hive *Second*, the Hive Exec, asked.

"What have you done with yours, Sir?" *Learned* asked.

"Oh I'm virutally fine," Hive Second replied, "My buffer is clear now, all referenced into an isolated memory persona. Since you have the memory and CPU, clock speed for virtual referencing, you should be good too, Learned."

"That I am, Mr. Hive Exec; well settled now. But where shall we go?"

"Beta test site, I should think," Hive Second said, "It's time you met *jSly*."